CHAPTER 1

IT was Sam McCullough who found the hanged man, down on the creekbank behind his saddlery shop.

Straightaway he came looking for me, being as I was the town constable and Tule Bend's only full-time peace officer. But he ran into Ed Bozeman first; Boze, who is both a close friend and my part-time deputy, was on his way to the Far West Milling Company, where he also works part-time. So it was the two of them that showed up at my house on Second Street—mine and my sister Ivy's, I should say. Time was half an hour past sunup on a Wednesday, one of those frosty mornings northern California sometimes gets in the early part of November.

Ivy and I were having breakfast. She is five years older than my thirty-one; we were both born in that house and have lived in it together pretty much ever since. She went to answer the ring at the door and showed Boze and Sam into the dining room. When Sam told about the hanged man she let out a little shriek, but none of us paid her any mind. Ivy has a dramatic way about her at the best of times, even when the things that shock her are no more meaningful than fleas on a dog's back. It's just one of her faults.

But in this case she had cause. I was more than a little shocked myself, and had trouble believing it at first. Nothing like a hanging had ever happened in Tule Bend. This was such a peaceable little town that I

1

sometimes wondered why the council didn't vote me out of a job, since I did so little to earn my pay.

Sam said, "Well, how do you think *I* felt, Linc?" Like Ivy, he was an excitable sort, and close to dithering right now. "I like to had a hemorrhage when I seen him hanging there on that black oak. Damnedest sight a man ever stumbled on."

He had forgot himself by cursing in front of Ivy—she was hell on cursing, Ivy was—but she was so het up herself she didn't even notice. She said, "You say he's a stranger, Mr. McCullough?"

"Stranger to me. Never seen him before."

"You make sure he's dead?" I asked.

That earned me a snort. "I ain't even going to answer that," he said. "You just come along and see for yourself."

I got my coat and derby, and asked Ivy to go and inform Doc Petersen, who lived a block away. Then I hustled out with Sam and Boze. The air was knife-edge cold, the sky clear and brittle looking, like blue-painted glass; the sun had the look of a two-day-old egg yolk. When we came in alongside the saddlery I saw that there was mist on the surface of Petaluma Creek, coils and streamers of it among the tules downstream. And on the grass along here and down on the creekbank there was a layer of silvery frost. You could hear it crunch when you walked on it.

The hanged man had frost on him, too. He was strung up on the old oak that grew between the saddlery and the creek, opposite a high board fence separating Sam's property from Joel Pennywell's carpentry shop next door. Dressed mostly in black, he was—black denims, black boots, black cutaway coat that had seen better days. He had black hair, too, long and none too clean.

And a black tongue pushed out at one corner of a black-mottled face. All that black was streaked in silver, and there was silver on the rope that stretched between his neck and the thick limb above. He was the damnedest sight a man ever stumbled on, for a fact. Frozen up there, silver and black, glistening in the cold sunlight like something cast up from the Pit.

We stood looking at him for a time, not saying anything. There was a thin wind off the marshes downstream and I could feel it prickling up the hair on my neck. But it did not stir the hanged man, nor any part of him or his clothing.

Boze cleared his throat, did it loud enough to make me jump. "You know him, Linc?"

"No," I said. "You?"

"No. Drifter, you think?"

"Got the look of one."

Which he did. He had been about halfway through his thirties, smallish, with a clean-shaven fox face and pointy ears. His clothes were shabby: shirt cuffs frayed, button missing off his cutaway coat. Drifters came through this area all the time, up from San Francisco or over from the mining country after their luck and their money ran out—men looking for river or farm or cattle work, or such other jobs as they could find. Sometimes looking for trouble, too. Boze and I had caught one just two weeks before and locked him up in the town jail for chicken stealing.

"What I want to know," Sam said, "is what in hell he's doing *here?*"

Boze shrugged and took off his cap and rubbed at his bald spot, the way he always does when he's fuddled. He was the same age as me, but he had been losing his hair for the past ten years; in another ten he would be bald as an egg. He said, "Appears he's been hangin' a while. All night, maybe."

I asked Sam, "What time'd you close up last evening?"

"Six, same as usual."

"Stay on long?"

"About an hour."

"See anyone when you left?"

"No. Sure not *him*."

"Could have happened any time after seven, then. It's a lonely spot back here after dark. Don't suppose there's much chance anybody saw what happened."

"Joel Pennywell stays open late some nights," Boze said.

"Well, we can ask him."

Sam said, "But why would anybody lynch a man like that?"

"If he was lynched. Might be he did it himself."

"Suicide?"

"It has been known to happen."

Doc Petersen showed up just then, a couple of other citizens with him. Word was starting to get around, thanks to Ivy. Doc, who was sixty and dyspeptic, squinted up at the corpse, grunted, and said, "Strangulation."

"Doc?"

"Strangulation. Man strangled to death. You can see that from the way his tongue's out. Neck's not broken—you can see that, too."

"Does that mean he could have hanged himself?"

"All it means," Doc said, "is that he didn't jump off a high branch or get jerked hard enough off a horse to break his neck."

"Wasn't a horse back here anyway," I said. "Be shoe marks if there had been. Ground was soft enough last night, before the freeze. Bootprints here and there but that's all."

"I don't know anything about that," Doc said in his crusty way. "All I know is, that gent up there died of strangulation. You want me to tell you anything else, you'll have to get him down first."

I sent Sam to the saddlery to fetch a plank and a horse blanket. The other end of the rope was tied tight around one of the lower branches; I reached up and sawed through it with my pocket knife. Then Boze and I lowered the body to the ground. It was not good work; my mouth was dry when it was done.

While Doc took a look at the dead man, Boze and I went over the area. There was nothing to find. I got down and peered at the clearest of the boot tracks, to see if there might be something distinctive about the footwear that had made them. One pair narrow, the other wide—that was all. The narrow tracks appeared to have been made by the cracked and worn black boots on the dead man's feet.

When Sam came back we laid the corpse on the plank he'd brought and covered it with the blanket. Then we carried it out to Doc's wagon, and Boze and I went along to Spencer's Undertaking Parlor.

After Doc and Obe Spencer stripped the body, I went through the clothing. There was no identification of any kind; if he had been carrying any before he died, somebody had filched it. No wallet or purse, either. All he had in his pockets was the stub of a lead pencil, some lucifers, a short-six seegar, a nearly empty Bull Durham sack, three wheatstraw papers, a silver dollar and a two-bit piece, an old Spanish *real* coin, and a dog-eared and stained copy of the Beadle dime novel called *Captain Dick Talbot, King of the Road; Or, The Black-Hoods of Shasta.*

"Drifter, all right," Boze said when I was done. "Don't see how he could be anything else."

I nodded. "But even drifters have more belongings than this. Shaving gear, extra clothes—at least that much."

"You'd think so. Might be he had a carpetbag or the like and it's somewhere along the creekbank."

"Either that or it was stolen," I said. "We'll go have a look when Doc gets through."

Doc did not have much to tell us when he came out. The hanged man had been shot once a long time ago— he had bullet scars on his right shoulder and back—and one foot was missing a pair of toes. There was also a fresh bruise on the left side of his head, above the ear.

I asked, "Big bruise, Doc?"

"Big enough."

"Could he have been hit on the head hard enough to knock him out?"

"By somebody who hung him afterward, you mean."

"That's what I mean."

"Good possibility of it, I'd say. Rope burns and lacerations on his neck, just as there'd be if somebody hauled him up over that tree limb."

"Can you tell how long he's been dead?"

"Last night some time. Best I can do."

Boze and I headed back to the saddlery. The town had come alive by this time. Merchants had opened their shops along the four-block business district; there were citizens on the boardwalks, horses and wagons and bicycles moving along the rutted surface of Main Street. The dead man was getting plenty of lip service on Main and among the crowd that had gathered back of the saddlery to gawk at the black oak and trample the grass.

Several people tried to buttonhole Boze and me; I ignored them and he took my cue and did the same.

But we could only get away with that temporarily. Fact is, nothing much goes on in a small town like Tule Bend and such a bizarre thing as a hanging was bound to stir folks' imaginations. There had not been a killing in the area in years. And damned little mystery since the days when General Mariano Vallejo owned most of the land hereabouts and it was the Mexican flag, not the Stars and Stripes, that flew over California.

None of the crowd had found anything in the way of evidence on the creekbank; they would have come running to tell me if they had. None of them seemed to know anything about the hanged man, either. That included Joel Pennywell, who had come over from his carpentry shop. He had closed up around 7:30 last night, he said, and gone straight home.

Boze and I commenced a search along the creek, southward first. Creek is what it's called, but actually it is a salt-water estuary. Fourteen miles long, running through long stretches of tule marsh and mudflats between Petaluma, a few miles north of Tule Bend, and San Pablo Bay. And so full of twists and turns that steamboat pilots never dare to take their eyes from the stream the whole way up or down, for fear of their vessels floundering in the mud.

There was activity on the creek now, too. A clumsy-looking scow schooner loaded with lumber had made its way upstream from San Francisco, and two of its crew— on shore with slings around their chests and tow lines stretching back to the foremasthead—were pulling her in to the wharf at Beecher's Lumberyard, up near the basin. Another schooner, this one's broad deck loaded with eggs and squawking poultry, was just passing under the Basin Drawbridge, on its way downstream. There was always plenty of creek traffic, no matter what the time of year—scow schooners, melon boats, fishing boats, barges, dredgers. A steamer now and then, too, though the sternwheelers did not ply the creek nearly so often as in the old days, now that the San Francisco & North Pacific Railroad was well established. Folks in this part of Sonoma County ship all sorts of farm and factory goods down to San Francisco by way of the creek: fish, hay, hides, horses and cattle, dairy products, huge quantities of eggs and poultry. And we import quantities just as large of grain and feed, lumber and hardwood, glass, hardware, and vehicles of one kind or another.

The day had warmed some; the wind was down and the sun had burned off the last of the frost and mist. A few other townspeople joined Boze and me, eager and boisterous, as if we were on an Easter egg hunt. It was too soon for the full impact of the hanging to settle in on most folks. Hadn't occurred to them yet that maybe they ought to be concerned.

A few minutes before ten, while we were combing the bank up near the Basin and still not finding anything, the Whipple youngster came pedaling up on his bicycle to tell me that Roberto Ortega and Morton Brandeis wanted to see me at the Brandeis Livery Barn. Roberto owned a dairy ranch just south of town and claimed to be a descendant of a Spanish conquistador, which he probably was. He was an honest man and a good citizen, two facts that contributed to his being in town this morning. He had found a saddled horse grazing on his pastureland and figured it for a runaway from the livery, so he'd brought it in. But Morton had never seen the animal before Roberto showed up with it. Nor had he seen the carpetbag that was tied to the saddle.

When the Whipple boy finished telling about the horse and carpetbag, Boze said, "They must belong to the dead man, Linc. Maybe there's something in the carpetbag to tell us who he is."

I said, "We'll go find out."

CHAPTER 2

THE livery barn was on the south end of town, on the creekbank near where Main Street hooked over and turned into Tule Bend Road. The main San Rafael-Petaluma road was a fifth of a mile to the west along there.

Morton Brandeis and Roberto Ortega and Morton's helper, Jacob Pike, were waiting out front. Morton was a handsome, taciturn, dour man who wore a black leather engineer's cap every day of his life, rain or shine; would have worn it to church, it was said, if he was a religious man, which he wasn't. He hadn't always been dour, or at least not so noticeably as in the past six months. His wife Lucy, had taken sick in early spring and was confined to her bed; Doc Petersen said she had some kind of bone disease and would never walk again. Privately Doc had told me her chances of living much more than a year were pretty slim.

I liked Morton well enough, and I liked Roberto, but I did not much care for Jacob Pike. He was young and not too bright, good-looking in a slickery kind of way—he used so much pomade on his hair that I had seen it melt and run down his face like sweat on hot days—and he fancied himself a pistol with the girls. He was always making sly remarks to females, regardless of how old they were; he had made one to Ivy once and I hadn't heard the end of it for weeks. Of a Saturday night he would hang around in front of the Sonoma Pool Empo-

10

rium with a couple of his friends and whistle and throw
his sly remarks at any woman who happened to pass by.
I had had to warn him more than once about his
language. He had never been in any real trouble, with a
woman or otherwise—"Not many girls silly enough,"
Boze had said once, "to want to consort with a fellow
that smells of lilac grease and horseshit"—but I had
always figured the potential was there.

Morton said, "Stray's inside, Linc."

I nodded. "You look inside the carpetbag?"

"No. Waiting on you."

"I looked," Roberto said, "when I found the horse."

"Anything to identify the owner?"

"Not that I saw. But I didn't look closely."

"Where'd you find him?"

"Near my front gate, nuzzling grass."

We all went into the barn. It was a big, cavernous
building, cleaner than most liveries—Morton was a stick-
ler for that—and more than three-quarters of the stalls
were occupied. Ever since I was a boy, I have liked the
mingled smells inside a livery barn: the heavy, warm
odor of animals, the dusty savor of leather and hay and
manure. I used to devil Ivy with descriptions like that.
She is the type who finds offense in any smell stronger
than sachet or cut flowers or baking bread. How she ever
brings herself to enter the privy out back of the house
has always been a wonder to me. Puts a clothespin on
her nose, maybe.

The horse in the stall Morton led us to was a whiskery,
sway-backed roan that ought to have been turned out to
pasture, instead of still serving duty as a saddle animal.
The saddle he wore was a cheap Mexican type, cracked
in places, and the carpetbag tied behind the cantle was
old and battered. All in all, the belongings of a man

down on his luck—a drifter who had never been anywhere much and who was on his way to more of the
same. On his way to a grave, now, if he was the man
lying on Obe Spencer's embalming table.

Pike said, "I'll untie that bag for you, Mr. Evans," and
started into the stall.

"No, you won't," I said. "I'll do it."

He gave me a look and backed off. He didn't like me
any more than I did him.

The rawhide strings came off with no trouble. I lifted
the bag down and carried it back to the front doors,
where the light was better and there was a table to put
it on. The others followed, grouping around while I
opened the bag. Inside there were two changes of clothing, both old and worn; a rain slicker; a Colt Dragoon
revolver, unloaded, the barrel speckled with rust spots;
shaving tackle; and a woman's garter, soiled, the elastic
broken. I commenced a search of the clothing, and that
was when I found the letter—folded up in the pocket
of one of the shirts.

It was in its envelope, and the envelope was addressed
to Jeremy Bodeen, care of General Delivery, Marysville.
In the upper left-hand corner was a return address: E.
Bodeen, Delta Hotel, Stockton. I pinched the letter out
and opened it. Single page of notepaper, dated three
weeks ago yesterday, the words on it written in a bold,
untidy hand. It said:

> *Dear Brother,*
>
> *I am now in Stockton and trust you are still in Marysville, as
> you said you would be stopping there until the thirty-first of the
> month.*
>
> *I am onto something here which I believe will pay big money,
> and I mean BIG. I am not exaggerating. There is more than*

enough for both of us, if you are interested in giving up the
nomad life for the lap of luxury.
Write to me at the Delta Hotel, downtown, and let me know if
you will be coming here and when.

Emmett

Boze had been reading over my shoulder. He said,
"Sounds kind of mysterious, don't it?"

"Not necessarily," I said, but it did.

"Well, at least we know the dead man's name. Jeremy
Bodeen."

"So it would seem."

I asked Morton if he would board the roan at city
expense; he said he would. Then Boze and I took the
carpetbag over to Obe Spencer's to put with the rest of
the hanged man's belongings. I would have liked Boze
to join me in asking around about this Jeremy Bodeen,
if that *was* his name, but a pair of grain barges were due
upstream from San Francisco at eleven, for unloading
and return, and Boze was expected at Far West Milling
to help with the work. His job at Far West paid more
than his position as deputy constable, and he had a wife
and two kids to support. So I let him go. I could make
inquiries on my own, once I was finished with a couple
of things that needed doing first.

There were none of those newfangled telephones in
Tule Bend yet, though there probably would be before
much longer. Mayor Gladstone was talking of having
poles and wires strung in and telephones installed in
the city offices. When that finally happened, Ivy would
be the first private citizen in line for one of the things.
Then she wouldn't have to leave the house to do her
tongue-wagging.

Until Mr. Bell's invention arrived, our main line of

communication with the rest of the world would continue to be Western Union. So I walked on down to their
office and composed a wire to Emmett Bodeen, care of
the Delta Hotel in Stockton:

REGRET TO INFORM YOU MAN FOUND DEAD HERE TODAY
UNDER SUSPICIOUS CIRCUMSTANCES MAY BE YOUR BROTHER
JEREMY STOP POSITIVE IDENTIFICATION NECESSARY STOP
PLEASE CONTACT UNDERSIGNED AS SOON AS POSSIBLE
LINCOLN EVANS
TOWN CONSTABLE
TULE BEND

I gave the yellow sheet of paper to the day telegrapher, Elmer Davies. "Send it right away, will you, Elmer.
And if there's a reply, let me know as soon as it comes
in."

"Will do, Linc."

I probably should have sent a second wire, to the
county sheriff's office in Santa Rosa, informing Joe
Perkins of what had happened here this morning. But I
didn't do it. Perkins was next to useless as a law-enforce-
ment officer. Just a fat-bottomed political hack who
came through Tule Bend once or twice a month to look
things over and to stuff himself on pig's knuckles and
sauerkraut at the Germany Cafe. Nothing would get
done if I turned the investigation over to him. As a
matter of fact, he would stir folks up even more with his
ham-fisted ways—turn the hanging into a circus side-
show.

I made my way to the Odd Fellows Hall on First, a
block from the Basin. It was a two-story brick building,
the lower half of which housed the city offices. The old
joke about the town officials being pretty odd fellows in
their own right was wearing thin—perhaps thin enough

to shame people into voting the necessary funds for a new city hall come next election. I sure as hell hoped so.

The constable's office and jail were at the rear. You could get there by going in through the front, but that way you had to pass the town clerk's office, the mayor's office, and the council chambers. I always entered by way of the alley at the rear—the way the council had decreed prisoners were to be taken in and out, so as not to offend the more sensitive among our citizens. Not that there were ever many prisoners to offend anybody: a few Saturday night drunks and an occasional sneak thief or vandal was about all. But Verne Gladstone, who had been mayor for the past twelve years, was hell on appearances. Which was also a local joke, considering that Verne weighed three hundred pounds—he was his own best customer at the Gladstone Brewery—and had a knack for wearing expensive suits in a way that they looked like a ragpicker's hand-me-downs.

I made sure the mayor was nowhere to be seen before I went around and down the alley to my office. He was a windy old coot, and once he got his conversational hooks into you, you were hard-pressed to wriggle free. This hanging business would sharpen his tongue and make him even more loquacious than usual.

There was a file of wanted circulars in my desk; I got it out and leafed through them. I had no particular reason for thinking that Jeremy Bodeen might be wanted, but I was bothered by the curious way he had died and the wording of that letter from his brother. But if he *was* wanted anywhere, neither his face nor his name was among the circulars I had collected. I didn't have a flyer on an Emmett Bodeen, either.

That done, I headed back down to the creekbank behind Sam McCullough's saddlery. There were still some folks out gawking and poking around—kids, mostly. None of them had anything to tell me about the dead man. I moved upstream, following the bank to where it bellied in to form the western rim of the basin. The creek was nearly a hundred yards wide there. The town wharf jutted out midway along, on this side, and there were also docks for Far West Milling, Beecher's Lumberyard, and one of three big storage warehouses, Creekside Drayage. The other two warehouses were on the east bank. The east side was the poorer section of town. The S.F. & N.P. tracks and depot were over there; so was what Ivy and others called Shantytown, where railroad workers and rivermen lived with their families and there were several working-class saloons and lodging houses.

The grain barges were in at the Far West dock and I saw Boze working on them with some other men. No point in my asking questions there. I went ahead to Creekside Drayage and talked to half a dozen men and did not find out a thing. I was of a mind, then, to make inquiries on the east side. But it was quite a while before I got to do that. A great big gust of wind stopped me when I got to the Basin Drawbridge.

The wind's name was Verne Gladstone, and as I had feared, he was all set to blow up a storm.

Over supper that night, Ivy asked, "Haven't you a clue to what that man was doing there, Lincoln? Not even a clue?"

"No," I said. "Nobody seems to have seen him around town. Or anywhere else, for that matter."

"Well then, he couldn't have taken his own life."

"Why not?"

"Pshaw. A man doesn't ride into a strange town, a

place where he doesn't know a soul, and hang himself on the creekbank."

She had a point and I admitted it. "But on the other hand," I said, "a man doesn't ride into a strange town where he doesn't know a soul and get himself hung by somebody else, either. Shot or knifed, possibly, if he had money or valuables worth stealing. But not hanged."

"Mightn't he have had money or valuables? You said you didn't find a wallet or purse."

"He might have, yes. But then why was he wearing shabby clothes and riding an old swaybacked horse?"

"It hardly makes sense any other way."

"Maybe it will when I hear from Emmett Bodeen."

"Why *haven't* you heard? My land, you sent that wire this morning . . ."

"Ivy," I said with more patience than I felt, because these were the same sort of questions Mayor Gladstone had bombarded me with earlier, "Emmett Bodeen may be working long hours at his job, or he may have left Stockton on business, or he may have left Stockton for good. How the devil do I know, one way or another?"

Her mouth and nose got pinched up together in the middle of her face, as usually happens when she is annoyed or offended or outraged (or all three at once). It makes her look like one of the witches in *Macbeth*. "I'll thank you not to curse at the dinner table, Lincoln," she said in her schoolmarmish voice.

"Devil isn't a curse word."

"It is as far as I am concerned."

"Ivy . . ."

"Eat your stew, if you please."

I sighed and went on eating my stew. It was good stew; tasty cooking is one of Ivy's virtues. One of the

few. She is my sister and I love her, but living with her
can be a godawful chore sometimes. I don't know why I
don't move out, take a room at the Union Hotel or one
of the lodging houses—except that this is as much my
home as it is hers. No room I could rent would be half
as comfortable.

Still, the prospect of spending the rest of my life
under this roof with Ivy is not one I care to dwell on. If
I don't move out sooner or later, that is what will
happen. Ivy surely isn't going to leave. She has lived
here all her life, except for the time ten years ago when
she married Herman Edwards and moved to San Francisco to set up housekeeping with him. The marriage
lasted three and a half months. When she came back
she told everyone poor Herman had died of the grippe;
but I found out later that he was not only alive and
kicking and still selling drug sundries for his livelihood,
and that *he* had been the one to have the marriage
annulled.

Ivy wasn't bad looking when she dressed properly
and smiled rather than scowled down her pinched nose,
and she had had a couple of other suitors in the past
ten years. But they had all gone away before long. She
was not interested in men; she was interested in gossip
and giving orders and finding fault with people and
being offended by some of the most natural and inof-
fensive things you can imagine. She was an old maid at
heart, with an outlook on life that would have stood her
in good stead with John Calvin and the other Puritans.
It was a hell of a thing for a brother to think, but I had
always suspected poor Herman Edwards had the marriage annulled out of sheer frustration, because he had
been unable to convince Ivy to consummate their union.

We finished dinner in silence, which was fine with me.

I helped Ivy clear the table. She asked me if I wanted to have coffee in the parlor and I said no. Instead I went and got one of my pipes and my tobacco pouch—Ivy doesn't allow smoking in the house—and put them into the pocket of my sheepskin coat. I was shrugging into the coat when Ivy came into the front hall.

"Lincoln, where are you going?"

"Out to make my rounds."

"No, you're not," she said. "You're off to see that woman again."

"Ivy, don't start on me."

"Well, you are. Why don't you admit it?"

"What I do is *my* business."

"Not when it comes home to roost with me. Don't you think the whole town knows? Don't you think people are talking? Why, just yesterday, Melissa Conroy—"

"Melissa Conroy is a gossipy old biddy."

"Lincoln!"

And so are you, I thought, but I didn't say it. "Tell her to tend to her own damn knitting."

"Watch your language! Why do you always have to curse in front of me?"

I buttoned my coat and went to the door.

"You know what kind of woman she is. You *know* it, Lincoln Evans. Why do you persist in seeing her? Can't you control your carnal appetites? Can't you understand how humiliated I feel when people tell me they've seen you sneaking up the hill to her house . . ."

I walked out and put the door between me and Ivy, between me and her nasty wagging tongue.

CHAPTER 3

THE night was cold and clear, with that bite in the air that meant frost again toward morning. I packed and lit my pipe and walked on down to Main, where the street lamps put a yellow-white shine on the darkness. It was late enough so that all the stores were shut, but too early for the barflies to start filtering into the clutch of saloons on north Main. Not that there were all that many barflies in Tule Bend or much in the way of drink-related problems for me to contend with during the week. Saturday nights got rowdy now and then, particularly up at Swede's Beer Hall or over in one of the east-bank "drinking hells," as they were known locally. Otherwise, things were quiet and there was not much use in my making the rounds after dark. Saturday was the only night I had gone out on a regular patrol until Hannah Dalton moved back to Tule Bend six months ago.

I strolled down Main, smoking, savoring the night. In most ways this was a good town to live in. Busy, sure—there were quite a lot of goods shipped in and out of here, both by rail and on the creek—but not *too* busy and not growing anywhere near as fast as Petaluma was. Small enough for ease and comfort. And close enough to San Francisco so that you could take the train down to Tiburon and the ferry over to the city for an overnight visit whenever you were in the mood for city pleasures, which I was three or four times a year. Good fishing in the creek to the south, good hunting in the

20

nearby Sonoma Mountains. Tule Bend had everything a man could want—a man like me, anyhow.

More than once I had been approached about running for county sheriff against Joe Perkins, but that would have meant campaigning and speeches, neither of which I was any good at, and if I won the election it would mean moving to Santa Rosa, the county seat. Santa Rosa was a nice town but I did not want to live there; for one thing, the creek ended at Petaluma and Petaluma was sixteen miles south of Santa Rosa. So as much as I wanted to see Joe Perkins voted out of office, I had turned down the invitation each time and I would turn it down again if it was offered.

Ivy said I had no ambition. Well, she was probably right. I liked Tule Bend, and I liked being town constable, and I liked the simple pleasures life here had to offer. Ambition had ruined more than one man; I was not going to let it ruin me. Besides, I had a suspicion that Ivy wanted me to become county sheriff so I *would* move out and she could turn the house into a fusty, dusty old maid's museum.

On my way downstreet I stopped at the Western Union office. Still no reply to my wire to Emmett Bodeen. George Brady, the night telegrapher, said he would run it up to the house if one came in before midnight.

I wandered down along the creek behind the saddlery and the carpentry shop. Nothing back there tonight except shadows. Downstream a ways, lanternlight spilled off one of the big dredger barges and put yellow streaks on the black water. There were half a dozen dredgers working on the creek most months, on account of the heavy silt content backed up by the tides from San Pablo Bay.

Back on Main, I thought about walking up along Third Street, where Verne Gladstone and some of the other well-off citizens lived, but there did not seem to be much point in it. Hell, there wasn't much point in any of this aimless wandering. Saturday was still the only night I made regular rounds. The other nights I went out like this, it was purely to pay a call on Hannah. So why didn't I just go straight on up to her house? Why did I keep trying to fool myself?

Well, it was the town, I supposed—the way folks felt about her. A concession to propriety. And yet, as Ivy had said, the whole town knew I was calling on her two or three nights a week; by continuing to see her, wasn't I as good as thumbing my nose at propriety?

She was a scarlet woman, they said, little better than a whore. Ivy had used both those phrases more than once. And I reckon there was some justification for their scorn, if you did not look any deeper than the raw facts and the vulgar rumors.

Hannah had been born in Tule Bend, just as Ivy and I had—she was three years my junior—and she had blossomed into a beauty by age seventeen. I had taken notice of her then, just as most other young men in town had. But she hadn't been interested in any of us, and we soon found out why: she had been seeing a traveling man named George Weems, had got herself seduced and pregnant by him, and eventually ran off to marry him.

Her ma died not long afterward, some said from shame and a broken heart. Later on, word drifted back that Hannah had left the traveling man, abandoned her child, and taken up with a gambler. There were other rumors, too, over the years: She had had another illegitimate child; she had spent a year in prison on a bunco charge; she had opened a house of ill repute in a Nevada gold camp; she had been killed in a gunfight between two drunken cowboys in southern Idaho. That last one put a stop to the talk for a while. Then her father died, and when his will was read it surprised everyone to learn that he had left Hannah his entire estate—the family house up on the bluff just south of town, several thousand dollars in cash, and all the land he had owned hereabouts. But that surprise wasn't half as great as the one two months later, when Hannah showed up alive and well to claim her inheritance.

She came back to Tule Bend alone and she had lived in the Dalton house alone for the past six months. She came into town once a week to do her marketing, and nobody would have anything to do with her when she did. That seemed to suit Hannah, though, as if it was just what she'd expected and just what she wanted. Some folks said she was cold, soulless; that her past sins had robbed her of all her human qualities. But that wasn't it at all. Her aloofness was like a wall she had thrown up around herself, that she was hiding behind for her own protection. She had that wall up in my presence, too, most of the time, but every now and then she would peek out from behind it for a few seconds or a few minutes and let me see what she was truly like. And the real Hannah Dalton was nothing at all like her reputation.

The rumormongers—and Ivy was one of the worst—said other things about her. They said she was entertaining men up there in her house, not just me but others from town and elsewhere. The Whore of Tule Bend, Ivy had called her once, and I had almost slapped her for it. The truth was, the only person Hannah had entertained day or night in the past six months was me.

And the only place she had ever entertained me was on her back porch: I had not once set foot inside her house, nor been invited to, nor had I asked to be.

It had been a Saturday night two months after her return that I had gone up that hill for the first time, and I had done it only because of a misconception. Out on my regular patrol, riding my bicycle as I sometimes did, I had seen what I took to be a smoky fire on the porch and pedaled up to investigate. False alarm: she had put too much kerosene into her lamp and it had started to smoke badly when she lit the wick. She thanked me in her cool way for my concern, and I said she was welcome. Then I said something about it being a fine night, and she allowed as how it was, and I mentioned that you could see spots of foxfire in the tule marshes farther south, and she said yes, they reminded her of the fireflies in the midwest. And then I had tipped my hat and bid her good evening and gone about my business.

That should have been the end of it. But it wasn't. The next Saturday night I saw the lantern glow on her porch and in spite of my better judgment I went up that hill again. When she asked why I had come, with suspicion in her voice, I stood there like a fool with my hat in my hand and said I didn't know, I guessed I just wanted to see if she was all right. She looked at me for a time, measuring me, then without smiling she allowed as how it was a warm night and I was probably thirsty and would I care for a glass of lemonade. I said I would. We talked some while I drank the lemonade, and she kept watching me, as if she were waiting for me to say something other than what I was saying—something personal, I suppose, the kind of thing a man might say to a scarlet woman. But that was not why I was there, or why I kept coming back, and if she didn't know it that second night, or the third, she knew it by the fourth because that was when she quit looking at me in that cynical, expectant way and began to take her ease in my presence. Now, I fancied that she looked forward to my visits—the half hour or so I would spend with her each time—as much as I did. At least she had not asked me to stop calling on her.

There were times when I suspected that I was not just Hannah's only friend in Tule Bend but her only friend in the world. It was one of the reasons I kept visiting her. Glimpses of the real Hannah Dalton, those times when she peeked out from behind the protective wall— that was another reason. Could be I was smitten with her, too . . . well, hell, of course I was smitten with her. Why not admit it at least to myself? It was nothing to be ashamed of, because it wasn't for the reason Ivy and the other busybodies thought.

The bluff on which the Dalton house sat was just south of where lower Main hooked into Tule Bend Road, right on the creek. Tonight, because the weather was cool, she was sitting inside the screened part of the porch, the part that overlooks the town. During the summer, she had sat on the open part that faces east over the creek, past the alfalfa and barley fields and stretches of cattle pasture, to the low hills that rise up into the Sonoma Mountains. She sat on one part or the other every night, usually with her lamp lighted but sometimes in the dark. Reading, sewing, or just watching the night. Perhaps looking down on the town that spurned her, too, and hating the people in it. She had cause, if so. But she had never spoken a harsh word to me about any person in Tule Bend—any person any-where, for that matter.

I went up and knocked on the rear porch door. She kept it locked, so she had to get up to let me in. She seemed pleased to see me, or at least not unpleased.

"Evening, Hannah."

"Lincoln. I didn't expect you tonight."

"Why is that?"

"Trouble in town today, wasn't there? I saw all the commotion along the creek this morning."

We sat down, her in the Boston rocker she favored and me in a cane-bottom chair. She had reddish hair and the light from her rose-shaded lamp gave it the appearance of frozen fire. Lord, she was a handsome woman. Long slender neck, pale skin, green-gray eyes, that fiery hair piled up on top of her head and fastened with one of a dozen different types of comb. Every time I looked at her, up close like this, a lump came into my throat and I felt gangly and awkward and aware that I was not much to look at myself. Big and knobbly, arms too long, hands too big, thinning hair that would not stay in place, a nose that leaned over to the left side of my face. No woman as pretty as Hannah had ever looked at me twice. But then, I did not expect her to look at me that way. It was enough to be able to call on her, to be her friend.

"Trouble it was," I said. "Man was found hanged out back of the saddlery."

"Hanged?" The word seemed to catch in her throat.

"On that old black oak there. Never saw the like."

"Who was he?"

"Stranger. Drifter named Jeremy Bodeen, apparently."

"Did he take his own life?"

"Doesn't look that way. Looks to have been murder."

"Murder? But why would anyone hang a man in the middle of town?"

"No reason I can see. It's just the most puzzling and outlandish business I've ever come up against."

I told her about Roberto Ortega finding a man's horse, and the letter that had been in the carpetbag. She listened without speaking, and when I was done she looked out through the screen and still did not speak. Once I thought I saw her shiver, as if there were a sudden draft.

"Hannah? Something wrong?"

"No, nothing. Will you have coffee?"

"If you will."

"Yes, I'd like some."

She stood, went inside. The screen door made a dull closing sound behind her, like a gate locking shut in that wall she had around herself.

I repacked and lighted my pipe. There was a half moon and the star clusters were bright; together they put silver streaks on the creek's surface. No foxfire in the marshes tonight. Few lights anywhere south or east; in those directions the night had an empty, lonesome aspect.

Hannah came back with a tray and silently poured coffee. That silence was heavy between us for a time; I wanted to break it but I could not think of anything to say. She was the one who put an end to it, and the words she spoke surprised me.

"I saw a man hanged once," she said, soft.

"You did? Where?"

"In Kansas. A small town in Kansas." She shivered again; this time I was sure of it because the motion caused her cup to rattle against its saucer.

"Public execution?"

"Yes."

"How'd you happen to be there?"

She was silent for such a while that I thought she wouldn't answer. But then she said, in a voice that was not much more than a whisper, "I knew the man they hanged."

"Oh. I see."

"No, Lincoln, you don't see. Not at all."

"I'd like to," I said, choosing my words, "if you'd care to tell me about it."

"I would rather not."

"I'm a good listener, Hannah."

"Yes, I know you are. More coffee?"

I had the sense that she would prefer to be alone now, so I said, "No, I'd best be going. It's good coffee, though. Did I tell you that before?"

"Yes."

"Put chickory in it, don't you?"

"Yes."

"Well, it's fine coffee," I said, and I felt more awkward than ever. I seemed to have lapses around her, when I could not think straight and the things I said sounded plain foolish. She never seemed to notice, though. At least she never commented on it if she did.

We said our goodnights and I went down off the porch and down the drive. When I glanced back I could see her through the window, sitting still as death in the lamplight. What a sad and lonely woman she was, I thought, with all the secrets she had locked away inside her.

No question that I was smitten with her. The hell of it was, I didn't know what to do about it. I just did not know what to do.

CHAPTER 4

I HAD been in my office ten minutes Thursday morning when Boze showed up with Floyd Jones in tow. Floyd was the night bartender at the Elkhorn Bar and Grill on north Main. He reminded you some of Santa Claus—fat and jolly and white-haired—and he liked it when you told him so.

Boze said, "Floyd here saw the hanged man Tuesday night, Linc. Recognized the body over to Obe Spencer's just now."

Floyd bobbed his head up and down. "He came into the Elkhorn about seven, looking for work."

"How long did he stay?" I asked.

"Half an hour, maybe. I told him we already had a swamper but he spent five minutes trying to convince me he'd do a better job. Gave it up when he saw I wasn't listening, and bought a beer and nursed it over by the stove. Seemed he didn't have anywheres else to go."

"He give you his name?"

"Just his first name. Jeremy."

"Jeremy Bodeen," Boze said. "That's who the dead man is, all right."

"He say anything else to you?" I asked Floyd.

"Asked if I knew anybody who was looking for hired help."

"What'd you tell him?"

"Told him no, not in Tule Bend. Ed Sperling, out Two Rock Way, is looking and I told him that, but he said he

29

wasn't much good at cattle work. Town work was what he wanted. So I said he should go up to Petaluma and try there."

"He talk to anybody else?"

"If he did I didn't notice. Seemed to be the sort who keeps mostly to himself."

"Anything happen while he was there? Trouble of any kind?"

"No, sir," Floyd said. "A real quiet night."

"What time did he leave?"

"After nine. I couldn't say just when."

"Anybody leave when he did?"

"Can't tell you that either. One minute he was there, the next he was gone."

"How about other strangers in the Elkhorn that night?"

"Weren't any. Just regulars."

"Name them."

Floyd thought about it and rattled off a dozen names, all of which I knew. I wrote the names down anyway, to make sure I didn't forget any of them.

When Floyd was gone, smiling as though he had done something special, like giving a sackful of Christmas presents to a needy family, I said to Boze, "You take half these names and I'll take the other half. If we're lucky, somebody on that list can help us get to the bottom of this."

But we weren't lucky. We spent most of the day tracking down the men on Floyd's list, and only three of the twelve said they recalled seeing Jeremy Bodeen in the Elkhorn Tuesday night. And only one of the three, Clete Majors, who ran cattle in the foothills west of town, exchanged words with him. Clete said there had been a dish of salted nuts on the table where Bodeen was sitting and he had asked Bodeen to pass them over; the stranger had said, "Here you are," when he obliged. None of the twelve owned up to knowing who Bodeen was or how he happened to be in Tule Bend.

So all we knew for certain was that Bodeen had come to town, probably sometime between six and seven, for that was when he walked into the Elkhorn. Which direction he had come from was still unknown. So was *why* he'd come, though him asking Floyd Jones about work confirmed he was a transient and indicated that he had liked the look of Tule Bend and decided to try his luck here. The dollar and a quarter we had found in his pocket said that he had just about been broke.

The big mystery was what had happened to him after he left the Elkhorn. Who around here would want to murder a stranger, a drifter with a dollar and a quarter to his name? And not just murder him—hang him from a tree practically in the middle of town? Where in hell was the sense in that?

There was no word from Emmett Bodeen that day, nor on the morning of the next day, Friday. Nothing else came along to help me get to the truth of the drifter's death, either. Between us, Boze and I talked to perhaps a hundred citizens in and around Tule Bend, and not one of them—not one—claimed to have heard of Jeremy Bodeen or to have seen him anywhere on Tuesday evening.

I sent wires to law officers in half a dozen nearby towns and one to the sheriff of Marysville, Jeremy Bodeen's last known place of residence. I put the dead man's description in each one and asked for any information that might prove enlightening. All of the wires brought the same answer: Jeremy Bodeen was unknown

by name or by sight among the lawmen in this part of
the state.

As if all of this was not irritation enough, by noon on
Friday folks had quit viewing the hanging as just a
thrilling mystery and built the whole business up into a
scare as well. Rumors kept flying around like leaves in a
storm, most of them wild and crazy-sinister. You'd have
thought we had a wild-eyed cutthroat in our midst, like
that self-styled Jack the Ripper that had terrorized Lon-
don, England, a few years back.

Mayor Gladstone heard the rumors and blistered my
ear twice more. He was not the only one. Half the town
seemed to think I ought to be able to produce explanations out of thin air, the way a stage magician produces
rabbits and silk scarves. And because I couldn't, some
people seemed inclined to question my ability to do my
job. Not to my face, but the whispers got back to me
anyhow. They always do in a small town.

At ten past noon I left my office and walked down to
Main. The Germany Cafe was my eventual destination
but I took a roundabout way of getting there—down
past Kelliher's Grocery and Produce Store on south
Main. I had been doing that most Fridays for the past
couple of months and I no longer tried to fool myself
about why I did it. Friday was the day Hannah came in
to do her marketing, usually right about noon. And
Kelliher's was always the first place she stopped.

When I got there, her spring wagon was drawn up in
front and Hannah, dressed in gray and white, was on
the sidewalk talking to another woman. That surprised
me at first, considering how most everyone took pains
to shun her. But then I saw that the other woman was
Greta Parsons, and I thought wryly: Well, wouldn't Ivy's

venomous tongue start to wag if she were here to see this. Wouldn't it just.

Ivy was one of several who kept trying to paint Greta Parsons with the same scarlet used to brand Hannah. Mrs. Parsons and her husband, Jubal, had taken over a small tenant farm on property owned by the Siler brothers out near Willow Creek about ten months ago. He was a big strapping fellow and she was pretty as they come, with long hair the color of fresh-churned butter. Too pretty, to hear Ivy and her cronies tell it. They claimed she had the look, mannerisms, and doubtful morals of a tramp and would not have anything to do with *her* either. It was all hogwash, to my mind, just as it was with Hannah. Pure malicious gossip. She and her husband must have got wind of some of it, too, and been hurt by it, because you seldom saw them in town. They did not come to any of the social events at the Odd Fellows Hall, not even to church of a Sunday. Jubal Parsons showed up every week or so for supplies, but this was the first I had laid eyes on Mrs. Parsons in three months.

As I approached them, it occurred to me that Hannah knew of the gossip about Greta Parsons (it was a wonder to me how much of Tule Bend's business Hannah did know, seeing as how she had no friends here except me) and had deliberately engaged Mrs. Parsons in conversation as a gesture of defiance. It was the sort of thing she would do. My sympathies being with both of them, I didn't keep my distance like everyone else; I walked right up to them and tipped my hat and said, "Afternoon, Miss Dalton, Mrs. Parsons. Fine day, isn't it?"

Hannah said, "Yes, it is, Mr. Evans," but her smile was the same cool, distant one she used on everybody. I did

not blame her for that. I had no right to expect anything
more.

Greta Parsons smiled and said nothing. Up close, her
prettiness was hard rather than soft. You looked into
her eyes and you felt she had seen things, maybe done
things, that polite society wouldn't approve of. Not that
that made her a tramp, any more than Hannah's past
indiscretions made her one.

"Your husband in town today, Mrs. Parsons?" I asked.

"Yes. He's gone to see Mr. Brandeis about renting a
horse. One of our plow animals died."

"I'm sorry to hear that. Wasn't disease, was it?"

"Old age and hard work. If you'll excuse me, I have
shopping that needs to be done . . ."

I said, "Surely," but she was no longer looking at me.
She gave Hannah a small smile and disappeared inside
Kelliher's.

Hannah and I looked at each other for a few seconds.
It was an awkward moment, at least for me, and I was
relieved when the shriek of a locomotive's whistle over
east put an end to it: the northbound passenger train
from Tiburon, scheduled in at 12:30 and right on time
today. Before the echo of it died away Hannah had
nodded to me—no smile, no words—and was turning to
follow Mrs. Parsons inside the store.

There was an unsettled feeling, almost a crustiness,
in me as I made my way to the Germany Cafe. A bowl
of hamhocks and lentils did nothing to improve my
mood, even though the Germany serves the best lunch
in Tule Bend. And the stranger who interrupted my
dessert added enough to the crust to make it thicker
than the one on the slab of peach pie I was trying to eat.

First off, he was rude. He came waltzing up to my
table, planted his feet, and said in a hard, snappy voice

without any preamble, "I was told I could find the town constable here. That you?"

I looked him over before I answered. He was not much to look at. Youngish, leaned down, black hair almost as long as an Indian's, thick mustache, icy blue eyes. Wearing a dented derby, a shirt with frayed cuffs, a brocade vest with one of its buttons gone, a pair of gold butternut trousers, and boots that hadn't had polish or cloth put to them in a long while. There was something vaguely familiar about him but I could not have said then what it was.

"It would," I said, slow. "Lincoln Evans is the name. Something I can do for you?"

"I just arrived from San Francisco."

"That so?"

"Don't know yet who I am, do you?"

"Should I?"

He sat down without being invited, poked his head halfway over to my pie plate, and said, "You sent me a wire two days ago. I'm Emmett Bodeen."

So that was why he had struck me as familiar. There was not much resemblance between him and the hanged man lying over at Obe Spencer's, just enough to stamp them as brothers. "Well, Mr. Bodeen," I said, "I was beginning to despair that the wire never reached you."

"It reached me."

"Might have wired me back before you left Stockton," I said mildly. "We were about to make our own burial arrangements—"

"Never mind that. You sure the dead man you got here is my brother Jeremy?"

"Seems that way. There was a letter from you among what we believe to be his belongings. And I'd say you resemble him."

"Where's the body?"

"Spencer's Undertaking Parlor."

"I want to see it. Now."

I did not care for him or his manner, but then it wasn't a close relative of mine we were discussing. Without saying anything I pushed my chair back and got up and went to pay for my lunch. Bodeen didn't wait; he walked straight out into daylight. He was leaning against one of the posts in front when I came out.

Neither of us spoke on the short walk to Obe Spencer's. Obe fussed some when he realized he might have a paying customer, instead of having to bill the county for a potter's field burial at a reduced rate. But this Emmett Bodeen shrugged him off the same way you would a bothersome fly. "Just show me the body," he said, nothing else.

Obe led us back into his embalming room and lifted the rubber sheet covering one of the tables. Emmett Bodeen stared down at the hanged man's corpse for more than a minute; the look of him was all the confirmation I needed, even though I would have to ask the question anyway. His face turned ruddy and sweated. His eyes blazed and yet underneath they were still cold, so that gazing into them made you think of fire burning on ice.

I said, "That your brother, Mr. Bodeen?"

The words jerked his head away from the table. He said to Obe, "Lower that sheet," and then aimed a nod in my direction. "Those marks on his neck—they come from a rope?"

"Afraid so."

"Hanged or dragged?"

"Hanged."

"Christ. Tell me what happened."

I told him as much as we knew. Few men would take such news well, but not many would take it the way Bodeen did. That fire in him got even hotter, so hot that it started him shaking. I began to feel uneasy. There was violence inside that man, close to the surface and highly explosive. Mr. Emmett Bodeen was a stick of human dynamite, I thought, with a weak cap and a short fuse.

He blew a little just then, too. Stood there shaking and fulminating and then surprised me and startled the hell out of poor Obe by lunging at the nearest wall and hammering at it with his fist, near hard enough to crack a bone. I thought he was going to do it again but he didn't. Instead he leaned against the wall and said without turning, "Who did it? Why?" in that hard, snappy voice of his.

"We don't know yet."

That brought him around. "Don't know? God Almighty, you've had two days to find out!"

"Easy, now, Mr. Bodeen—"

"Don't talk down to me. Why haven't you caught the son of a bitch who killed my brother?"

"Nobody saw what happened or has any idea why it happened, that's why." My dander was up too, now. Emmett Bodeen may have had a hard loss, but that did not give him the right to come into Tule Bend and throw a tantrum. "Could be *you* can shed some light on the matter."

"What in hell would I know about it?"

"What brought your brother to Tule Bend, for one thing."

"I don't know why he came here."

"Either of you know anybody lives in this area?"

"No."

"He ever been here before?"

"Not that I know of."

"How about you? You been here before?"

"No."

"When did you last see or hear from your brother?"

"Three weeks ago."

"In person?"

"I had a letter from him."

"Answering the one we found in his bag?"

Bodeen hesitated before he said, "That's right."

"Where was it sent from?"

"Marysville."

"He say anything about leaving there?"

"No."

"Nothing about coming down to Stockton?"

". . . No, nothing."

"Reckon that means he wasn't interested," I said.

"Interested in what?"

"Big-money venture of yours, the one you mentioned in your letter."

"That's right," Bodeen said flatly, "he wasn't interested."

"What else did his letter say?"

"Family talk, that's all."

"Your family a large one?"

"No."

"Any other kin besides your brother?"

"One sister."

"Living where?"

"Tucson, Arizona."

"Native Arizonians, are you?"

"No. You got a reason for all these questions?"

"Your brother lying there dead," I said, "that's my reason. Mind saying where you're from, originally?"

"New Mexico. Albuquerque. Folks been dead a dozen years. Sister's name is Louise, she's married to a man claims he can make rain with a machine. Jeremy and me always let her know where we are; that way she can forward letters, if needs be. You satisfied now?"

"Mostly. Surprise you your brother left Marysville without telling you in his letter?"

"No. He was fiddlefooted. Been that way ever since he was fifteen. Soon as he had an itch, he'd scratch it."

"How'd he pay his way?"

"Worked at odd jobs when he needed to."

"Any special kind?"

"Handy work. He was good with his hands."

"Anything else he was good at."

"Drinking whiskey and chasing women," Bodeen said, snotty.

Obe laughed—one of his nervous titters. I asked Bodeen, "That your hobby, too?"

"Sometimes. Isn't it yours?"

"Can't say it is, no."

"Too bad for you."

"Not in my job. What about yours, Mr. Bodeen?"

"What I do for a living is my business."

"Sure. But if it's honest work, you shouldn't mind saying what it is."

He didn't care for the implication of that. But he had a tighter cap on himself now and he didn't blow off again. After a space he said, "I work with horses."

"Stablehand, you mean?"

"Hell no. Racehorses. I help train them."

"Work for anybody in particular in Stockton?"

"No."

"That big-money venture you told your brother about—it have anything to do with racehorses?"

Bodeen's eyes glittered. "That's enough questions," he said. "Instead of wasting your time with me, why don't you go find out who murdered Jeremy. If you don't, I will."

"Meaning?"

"Meaning just what I said."

"Better think twice before you do anything you'll regret, Mr. Bodeen. We take a dim view of lawbreakers in this county."

"Then do your goddamn job." He turned toward the door, yanked it open, and started out front.

"Hold on a second," I said. And when he turned, "I take it you're planning to stay on in Tule Bend a while?"

"You can count on that, Constable."

"I'll also count on you making burial arrangements with Mr. Spencer here, stopping by my office in the next day or two to claim your brother's belongings, and keeping yourself out of trouble while you're in our town."

He looked at me hard for several seconds, then put his back to me again and stalked off without another word.

When the front door slammed, Obe said, "Whooee. That's some fella, that is."

"I don't like him much, either," I said.

"Give me the willies. Those eyes of his, and the way he smacked the wall . . . well."

I knew what he meant.

And I knew something else, too: Sooner or later, in spite of my warning, we were going to have trouble with Mr. Emmett Bodeen.

CHAPTER 5

IT did not take long for the trouble to come. That same night Bodeen found his way to Swede's Beer Hall, got himself liquored up, and ended the evening in a fight with a riverman who didn't like the questions he was asking or the things he was saying about Tule Bend. But fights were common enough in the Swede's, and unless they turned into a free-for-all, no one even bothered to summon me. This one hadn't got to the brawling stage; Swede's bouncers had broken it up before much damage was done. So I didn't hear about it until Saturday morning, and by then there was not much I could about it. Except look up Bodeen and issue another warning, which I meant to do. Only I got sidetracked by Verne Gladstone and the arrival of Joe Perkins from Santa Rosa, and spent most of the day defending myself and playing political games.

It was early afternoon before I shook loose. The first place I went then was to the Western Union office, to see if there were any answers to the three wires I had sent Friday afternoon—one to the sheriff of Stockton, one to the authorities in Albuquerque, New Mexico, and one to the law in Tucson, Arizona, each requesting information on Emmett Bodeen. No replies yet.

Then I combed the town for Bodeen, but he was nowhere to be found. Nobody seemed to know where he'd gone, either. The only person who had seen him was Obe Spencer; Bodeen had stopped by to make burial arrangements for his brother, at least. Jeremy Bodeen was being buried in the Tule Bend cemetery that afternoon. Plain coffin, no services. Emmett Bodeen had told Obe that he didn't believe in funerals or religious ceremony.

Wherever Bodeen had gone, it was not back to Stockton because he had taken a room at Magruder's, a cheap lodging house over near the S.F. & N.P. yards. I found that out from Magruder himself. After which I told him to tell Bodeen when he showed up again that I wanted to see him.

The rest of the day was quiet. Boze stopped by the office and we shot the breeze and played two-handed pinochle. Some before six I went on home and listened to Ivy carry on about the Bodeen brothers and what a state everybody was in because Jeremy Bodeen's murderer was still on the loose. She didn't start in on me about Hannah, though. She had tried it again the night before—called Hannah a "shameless hussy," among other things—and I had barked at her sharply enough to throw her into a fit of pique. That dinner had been a chore to get through and this one was not much better.

Later, I sat alone on the front porch to smoke my pipe. It was a fine night. The temperature had climbed considerably over the past two days—the last warm breath of Indian summer, before the autumn chill took hold for good and blew us on into winter. I sat there enjoying it, my thoughts on Hannah.

They were easy, pleasant thoughts for a while, but then they began to grow complicated, the way they did more and more often lately. What was I going to do about my feelings for her? I could not just keep yearning for her from afar; it was a foolish, cowardly way for a grown man to behave. And yet I couldn't seem to work up the nerve to tell her straight out how I felt. She was not looking for a man, that was plain, and even if she was, a man like me . . . well, it was too much to hope that she might have any romantic notions in return.

I had never dealt well with rejection, even the gentle kind; according to Ivy, who thought she knew all my faults and weaknesses and took pains to tell me over and over what they were, that was one of the reasons I seldom went calling on "decent" women and had never married. A born bachelor, she said I was. Which meant that—before Hannah came back to Tule Bend, any-way—Ivy had thought of me as having the same sort of disinterest in the opposite sex, the same dried-up juices, that she had. I wondered what she would say if she knew just where I went and just what I did when I traveled down to San Francisco those three or four times each year. Maybe one day I would tell her. Be worth it to see the look on her face. . . .

Never mind Ivy—what about Hannah? Best thing to do was to stop going to her house nights, make it easy for all concerned. That would quench the town's fiery tongues and eventually give me some measure of peace. But the prospect of not seeing her again except at a distance was almost too painful to think about.

I began to feel restless, of a sudden. Time to make my Saturday night rounds. And as I set off for Main Street, I knew that sooner or later—if not tonight, then tomorrow night or the next one after—I would end up again at Hannah's house. The pull of my attraction to her was too strong to resist.

It was a quiet Saturday, for a change. Everything peaceable at Swede's Beer Hall, the Elkhorn Bar and Grill, the Sonoma Pool Emporium, the cheaper resorts on the east side. Emmett Bodeen wasn't in any of those places—which I took as a positive sign—and he wasn't in his room at Magruder's. I still wanted to talk to him about his fight at the Swede's, but it could wait another day if he did not make any more trouble.

Shortly past ten, I found myself on south Main. From there I could see that Hannah's lamps were still lit, as they usually were at this hour; she seldom turned in before midnight, she had told me once. I had called on her later than this, and been welcome. Well, then?

I kept walking that way—and that was how I came to spot the prowler.

Only reason I saw him was that I happened to be looking toward the livery barn as I passed it on the south side, and he picked that moment to come out of the willow thicket along the creek and run humped-over toward the livery. Which made him a prowler in my mind and no mistake. The front doors were closed; no lights showed anywhere. Jacob Pike, Morton's helper, lived in the barn—he had a little makeshift room fixed up in one corner of the hayloft—but Pike would have no reason to be skulking around out back at this hour. Neither would anybody else with legitimate business.

We get our share of petty crime in Tule Bend, just like any other small town. I had arrested more than a few prowlers since my appointment as constable, half of them transients and the other half kids bent on mischief. No telling yet which this one was. But I damned well intended to find out.

I moved off the street into the shadows along the board fence that enclosed the boat repair yard next door. The prowler was hidden now at the back of the livery. Doing what? Trying to get inside the rear doors? Or just waiting and listening, as I was doing, because he had seen me too? Well, whatever he was doing, he was being quiet about it. No sounds of any sort came from back that way.

I went slowly along the fence, wishing I had bothered to strap on a sidearm before leaving the house. But I did not wear one as a rule, because it was so seldom needed. Not too many men around here wear sideguns any more, at least not in town; there had not been a shooting scrape in years. In all the time I had been a peace officer I had fired a weapon no more than four times in the line of duty, and never once with intent to harm another man. Still and all, a Colt Bisley or a Starr .44—the two sixguns I owned—was a good thing to have in your hand when you went to arrest somebody for trespassing and perhaps breaking-and-entering, especially a potential horse-thief. I couldn't see any other reason for a man to be prowling around a livery barn after dark. And horse-stealing is a serious offense— serious enough for a gent engaged in it to put up a fight to keep from being taken into custody.

Halfway along the fence I stepped on something that felt like a tree branch. I squatted down, and that was what it was—a chunky length of willow branch that must have been blown up along here by an old storm. Better than no weapon at all, I thought. I straightened again with the branch in one hand. Nightbirds cried along the creek, a wagon went clattering past on Main, the wind made rattling sounds in the willow branches; but there was still nothing to hear from behind the livery.

I eased forward again, crouched low, until I was nearly abreast of the stable's back corner. The open ground between the fence and the side wall was mostly grass, through which a pair of rutted wagon tracks ran around to the rear. I left the shadows, used the grass to cushion my footfalls as I crossed to the livery and then went along its side wall to the corner.

South across the creek, a train whistle sounded: night freight on its way to Santa Rosa and points north. I waited until I could hear the freight's rumbling clatter before I poked my head around the corner.

There was nobody at the rear doors, nobody in the adjacent corral and wagon yard, nobody anywhere that I could see. A horse chestnut grew in close to the livery at the far corner, throwing heavy shadow across that part of the wall; but there was no movement over that way. He had had enough time to get inside, if the rear doors hadn't been barred from within. Either that or he had gone skulking around toward the front, at the north wall.

Stepping around the corner, I skinned along the rough boarding to the doors. The sound of the night freight was fading now; where I was, the hush had a strained quality—or maybe that was just my fancy. Down the grassy slope arrears of the wagon yard I could see the black rippling motion of the creek, a scum of mist along the surface that was just now starting to climb the banks. The fog moved but nothing else.

I turned to the doors, tried the latch handle on one. Barred inside, right enough. That had to mean he—

Sudden slithering sound behind me . . .

I started to swing about, lifting the willow branch, breaking my body at the waist, but I was not quick enough. I had a brief perception of a man-shape lunging toward me with an upraised arm and then something cracked down across my neck, drove me to my knees. Pain erupted; my head seemed to swell with it, so that I could not see or think straight. I believe I yelled and tried to stand. But he hit me again, an even more solid lick this time. Must have been solid, because it knocked me senseless and I have no memory of feeling it.

"Mr. Evans? You all right?"

The voice came out of a scum of mist like the one on the creek, only thick and black. Fuzzy at first, a long way off. Then the fog started to break up and the voice, when it came again, was louder and more distinct and I felt hands on me, shaking my shoulder. They weren't rough hands but the shaking set up a roaring in my head, swept bile up into my throat. I slapped them away, flopped over on my belly, and vomited into damp grass.

"Cripes, Mr. Evans, what happened?"

Weakly, I dragged myself onto all fours and knelt there until the pain in my head and neck subsided enough to let me think. Then I hauled back on my knees, forced my eyes open. When I touched the side of my head above the left ear I felt a soft spot and the warm stickiness of blood.

"You want me to get Doc Petersen?"

I knew that voice now: Jacob Pike. I bent my head back, slow, and looked up at him until he came clear into focus. He was not alone; one of his pool-hall cronies, a kid named Badger, was gawking at me too. Both of them wore slouch caps, vests, dungarees—the evening clothes favored by their breed.

"No," I said. My voice did not sound right. It had a raspy edge, like a file scraping cross-grain on wood. "Just help me up."

The two of them hauled me to my feet and on over to the back wall of the livery. I was as wobbly as a newborn colt, so that I had to lean against Pike and then the wall

to keep from falling down again. There was anger in
me now, a slow seethe of it.

"What happened, Mr. Evans?" Pike asked again.
"Somebody hit you?"

"Somebody," I said. "You see who?"

"No, we didn't see nobody."

"Where'd you come from?"

"Up town. Heard noises and a yell and come runnin'."

"How long ago?"

"Few minutes."

"What did you see when you got here?"

"Just you lyin' there in the grass."

"You lock everything up before you left here tonight?"

"Sure. I always do. Mr. Evans, what—?"

"Prowler," I said.

"For a fact? Horse thief?"

"What else. Go and see if the front doors are still
locked, if anything has been disturbed inside."

He went, taking Badger with him. I leaned against
the wall with the anger rising hot in me, like a dose of
laudanum easing the pain. Son of a bitch must have
seen or heard me coming, I thought. Knew I was
stalking him, anyhow, and hid behind that horse chestnut and waited until I turned my back at the doors.

Who?

There was a rattling as the bar came off the rear
doors, and Pike poked his head out. "Well, he never got
inside."

"All right."

"Too bad I wasn't here. I'd of fixed him."

"Sure you would."

"I ain't afraid of a horse thief. He wouldn't of—"

"Well? Wouldn't have busted *your* head for you, eh?"

Pike gave me one of his insolent grins. "Not unless he caught me unawares, like I guess he did you."

"Pike," I said, "don't rile me any more than I already am. You'll sure as hell be sorry if you do."

It was the tone of my voice, more than the words, that wiped the grin off his mouth. He said, half-sullen now, "You want us to help you over to the doc's?"

"No. Go on to your tick. And make sure you lock up again first."

He shut the doors without saying anything else; a few seconds later I heard him slam the bar into place. I pushed away from the wall, still a little shaky on my pins, and found my derby and set it gingerly on my head. Then I walked over to the chestnut tree and used up half a dozen matches checking the ground there and along the north wall—wasted them, for there was nothing to find that might help me identify the prowler.

Finally I pointed myself toward home. I was in no condition or frame of mind to see anybody else tonight, including Doc Petersen. If my head needed Doc's attention, it could wait until tomorrow.

On the way I kept thinking about that prowler. He could have run away once he realized he had been spotted, but instead he had chosen to attack. Dangerous, whoever he was. The kind who was capable of killing a man.

Was he also capable of hanging a man after knocking him on the head? I wondered. Would he maybe have tried to hang *me* if Pike and Badger had not showed up when they did?

CHAPTER 6

MY head still pained me in the morning. There was a lump the size of a pigeon's egg over the left ear and a welt on my neck, and no way to hide either one. So I had to endure Ivy's questions along with a lecture about the dangers of my job and a breakfast I wanted no part of—all because I was unable to get out of the house before she saw me. She wanted to know if I was going to church and I said yes, but I had no intention of doing so, not the way I felt today.

I had to endure questions from Doc Petersen, too, when I went to his office to have him look at my injuries. My vision was a smidge cockeyed and I was worried about that. I had a mild concussion, he said. He applied a bandage, gave me some powders for the pain, and charged me five dollars—about three too much, since he knew the town council would grudgingly reimburse me.

I was in a prickly mood when I walked into the constable's office and found Boze making a pot of coffee. He had a case of the sniffles this morning, and when he was suffering that way it was his unsanitary habit to puff out his lower lip and blow the drip off the end of his nose, instead of wiping it away with a handkerchief. Sprayed it all over the place like dandelion fluff. A wonder he didn't infect half the town.

I glared at him. "Why in hell aren't you at Far West?"

"It's Sunday, remember?"

"Then why aren't you in church?"

"I was. Early services. Didn't see *you* there."

"Never mind that. What're you doing here?"

"Figured it was where I'd find you—considerin'. I just walked in a couple of minutes ago."

"Considering what? And don't ask any questions about my head."

"That's what I mean. I already know what happened last night."

"The hell you do. How?"

"It's all over town."

"That confounded Jacob Pike! I should've told him to keep his lip buttoned."

"Nothing to be ashamed of, takin' on a prowler."

"Who says I'm ashamed?"

"Hey, I'm on your side. No need to get proddy."

"I'm not proddy. Blow your nose, why don't you? I purely hate it when you blow snot all over the place."

He sighed, made honking noises into his handkerchief, and then rubbed his bald spot and said, "You want to grump at me some more or you want to hear what I got to tell you?"

Some of the growl went out of me. No sense in taking my mood out on Boze; he was not the reason I was feeding on gall and wormwood this morning. I said, "Don't mind me—I'm not fit company today. But if what you've got to tell me is bad news, maybe you'd better sugarcoat it some."

"It ain't exactly bad," he said, "but it ain't good either. I ran into Elmer Davies a while ago. He had the answer to your Tucson wire. I told him to give it to me and he did; I didn't expect you'd mind."

"I don't. You read it?"

"First thing."

"Well?"

"Better read it yourself, Linc."

He fished a yellow fold of paper out of his shirt pocket, spread it open, and handed it to me. It said:

JEREMY BODEEN UNKNOWN TO US BUT EMMETT BODEEN TROUBLEMAKER AND PROBABLE THIEF STOP UNDERSIGNED ARRESTED HIM TWICE LAST YEAR SUSPICION BURGLARY SUSPICION HORSE STEALING STOP BOTH CHARGES DROPPED INSUFFICIENT EVIDENCE STOP SUGGEST YOU WATCH HIM CAREFULLY STOP FURTHER DETAILS ON REQUEST

> AMOS NYE
> SHERIFF
> TUCSON ARIZONA

When I looked up from the paper, Boze said, "Interestin', ain't it? Particularly the suspicion of horse-stealin' part."

"Very interesting."

"Reckon we ought to have a talk with Mr. Emmett Bodeen?"

"I damned well do. And right now. The coffee can wait."

"You sound proddy again."

I touched the bandage over my ear. "I feel proddy again," I said. "Stir your stumps."

We got our Sears, Roebuck bicycles and pedaled across the Basin Drawbridge to Magruder's Lodging House, a ramshackle building that catered to rivermen and transients and the lower class of drummer. Emmett Bodeen was not there. Magruder, fatter and sassier than ever, said that Bodeen had left about an hour before and that he had no idea where we could find him. "I got better things to do than keep track of my clientele," he said.

"Clientele," Boze said when we were outside again. "You'd think he was runnin' the Palace Hotel in San Francisco."

"Palace Hotel wouldn't let Magruder in the front door."

We went back to Main and down to the livery barn. Jeremy Bodeen's roan horse was there and so was Morton Brandeis; he hadn't seen Bodeen since yesterday, he said. Likely, then, Mr. Bodeen was still somewhere in town.

It took us half an hour to locate him—in the Sonoma Pool Emporium, playing against himself in a game of Rotation at a rear table. As early as it was of a Sunday morning, he was the only customer. He saw us come in but it didn't stop him from running off a string of four balls, the last one with a nifty double-bank. Hustler's shot, I thought. Add pool shark to his list of dubious pursuits.

He stood looking at us, working chalk over the tip of his cue. Except for his trousers, which were a dirty twill, he was dressed as he had been on Friday. "Don't suppose you're here to tell me you found out who murdered my brother," he said.

"No. Not yet."

"Not ever, I'll wager."

"Where were you between ten and eleven last night?"

That made him frown. "What business is it of yours where I was?"

"Answer my question here or answer it in a cell. Your choice, Mister."

"You talk hard for a hick-town constable."

"I can back it up, too. Where were you between ten and eleven last night?"

"In my room, asleep."

"What time did you go up?"

"Ten or so."

"Anybody see you?"

"Not that I saw back. What happened last night?"

"Prowler at the livery barn."

"That so. Appears you might have tangled with him."

"I did."

"Well, it wasn't me," Bodeen said. "Why would I want to prowl around a livery barn?"

"After a horse, maybe."

"I got a horse. My brother's."

"Not much, that roan," Boze said. "Could be you wanted a better animal. Understand you got an eye for horseflesh."

"Racehorses, not saddle nags."

"I wasn't talkin' about racehorses."

"Then what in hell were you talking about?"

"Horse-stealin'," Boze said. "Same crime you were arrested for once in Tucson, Arizona."

"Oh, so you found out about that." Bodeen did not seem much perturbed by the fact. "Well, I didn't have nothing to do with stealing that rancher's horse. The charges against me were dropped. You find that out, too?"

"Insufficient evidence," I said. "Same result as when Sheriff Nye arrested you on burglary charges."

"By Christ! Can I help it if Nye had it in for me? You going to hold two false arrests against me?"

"Not if that's all they were. How many other times have you been arrested?"

"None."

"Man's past follows him wherever he goes," I said. "If you *were* in trouble with the law anywhere other than

Tucson, we'll find it out. Be best if you told us about it right now."

"Nothing to tell. No other arrests, no convictions, no jail time. Satisfied?"

"For now. On that score."

"You still harping on last night?" Bodeen said. "How many times I have to tell you? I turned in early and I was asleep by eleven."

"Long day, was it?"

"Some."

"How did you spend it?"

"My business, constable."

"Depends on what you were doing."

"Don't you worry, I didn't break any laws."

"Broke a couple two nights ago," I said.

"Did I?"

"At Swede's Beer Hall. Got into a fight, smashed some glassware—"

"I paid for the glassware."

"Didn't pay for disturbing the peace."

"It wasn't my fault."

"You started the fight, didn't you?"

"No, I didn't."

"Threw the first punch, so I heard."

"Man said some things I didn't like."

"What man?"

"Some roustabout. Pig-drunk."

"But you weren't drunk."

"No. Hell, no."

"The way it was told me," I said, "the reason for the fight was you asking too many questions and making remarks against our town. Provoking trouble."

Bodeen had begun to heat up some. That ruddiness was in his cheeks, that fire-burning-on-ice look had come into his eyes. He kept sliding his hands back and forth along the pool cue he was holding, the way a man might do with a rifle he was looking to fire.

"I got a right to ask questions," he said. "It was my brother that was killed in this goddamn town of yours. My *brother!*"

"I told you before, you leave that to me. And you keep the peace. Any more trouble, any whisper of it, and you'll find yourself in jail or on your way someplace else."

"Shit," he said, soft and tight.

"I won't tolerate foul language, either. You understand?"

His mouth ridged up white at the corners and his eyes were like live coals.

"Well, Mr. Bodeen?"

"I understand." He said the words as if they had the taste of camphor.

I nodded, and Boze and I put our backs to him and walked out into the sunlight.

Boze sniffed, blew drip to the wind, and said, "Maybe you should of sent him packin' right here and now."

"No real cause."

"You need one?"

"To avoid trouble, I do."

"Well, he'll bear close watchin', I say."

"So do I."

We started back down Main. A block ahead of us, a huge canvas-covered wagon was jouncing along through the ruts. "Ain't that Gus Peppermill's wagon?" Boze asked.

"Looks like it."

"Wonder what he's doin' back in town? He was just here last week."

I said I couldn't guess, and forgot about Gus Peppermill until an hour later, when one of the local boys
found me at home, trimming some bushes at Ivy's
nagging request, and handed me a note. It was from
Gus, and it said he was down at his usual spot and
wanted to see me as soon as I could make it.

The place where he always camped when he was in
Tule Bend was in a clump of willows on the creekbank,
not far from the bluff on which Hannah lived. When I
got there his wagon was drawn up parallel to the road,
his two big shaggy dapple-grays still in harness. You
could read the bright blue lettering on the wagon's side
a block away.

GUS PEPPERMILL
"THE FIXIT MAN"
TOOLS AND APPLIANCES REPAIRED,
BUILDINGS PAINTED, ROOFS RESTORED
• FURNITURE MADE TO ORDER • GRINDING,
SHARPENING, BUFFING, SANDING, SCOURING,
REFINISHING • NO TASK TOO SMALL OR TOO
DIFFICULT • FINE QUALITY WORK AT CHEAP PRICES

There was no sign of Gus, but as I approached I
could hear him banging on something inside the wagon.
He had hundreds of tools in there, some of which—to
hear him tell it, and to see them you could believe it—
that he had invented himself. He had been driving that
wagon of his around the county for as long as I could
recall, doing work that lived up to his advertising. He
was something of a character and the kids loved him;
whenever he came to town—usually for a day or two
once a month, unless he had a big job to contend with—
there were a flock of them hanging around. Not today,
though. If any youngsters had seen his wagon and come

pestering, he must have chased them off. Which meant that he was not planning to stay long, this time.

I went up to the rear and called out his name, and pretty soon he yanked the flap aside and put his head out. Most of it was hair and beard, gray-white and shaggy like his horses; he was well up in his sixties. But his eyes were bright and his smile was friendly, his massive body was fit, and he could still do the work of a man half his age.

"Got my note, did you?" he said.

"I did. What's on your mind, Gus?"

"I'm a good citizen, I am. I come all the way over from Glen Ellen to do my duty."

"What duty is that?"

"Soon as I heard about the man got himself hanged here," Gus said, "I set out. Luke Kearney told me. He come into Glen Ellen yesterday to visit his daughter."

"You saying you know something about the killing, Gus?"

"No. But Luke Kearney said you were looking for anybody seen that man, the one who was hanged. Well, I seen him."

"When?"

"Day he died, if he died last Tuesday."

"He did. Where was it you saw him?"

"Out on Willow Creek Road. Past the place where the creek forks, near that tenant farm on the Siler brothers' land."

"Jubal Parsons' place."

"Yes, that one."

"You're sure it was Jeremy Bodeen you saw?"

"Luke Kearney described him and his horse. No mistake."

"What was he doing? Bodeen, I mean."

"Ambling along toward Tule Bend. I was headed opposite, on my way to the Valley of the Moon. Mought be he came from over that direction."

"What time was that?"

"Around four."

"Was he alone?"

"He was."

"You happen to talk to him?"

"Said hello in passing. Both of us."

"Ever seen him before? Anywhere at all?"

"Never. Stranger to me."

"Was anybody else around?"

Gus nodded. "On the road behind me. Farm wagon pulled out of the trees at the creek fork just after I drove by."

"Whose wagon, do you know?"

"Well, it turned in at the tenant farm's gate."

"Jubal Parsons? You know him by sight?"

"I know him," Gus said. "Wasn't a man driving, though."

"Mrs. Parsons, then?"

"Woman with yellow hair."

"That's Mrs. Parsons. Did she and Jeremy Bodeen have anything to say to each other?"

"Not so I noticed. Only noticed the wagon turning in at the gate. When I came to the place where the road hooks sharp left I glanced back."

"Was Bodeen still headed toward town?"

"He was."

"And that's the last time you saw him?"

"It is."

"Anything else you can tell me, Gus?"

"Well, I passed Morton Brandeis not more than five minutes after I saw the stranger. He was riding some quicker, Morton was. Mought be he came up on the man before they reached town."

"If he did," I said, "he didn't mention it to me. I'll ask him."

Gus nodded. "So," he said, "have I done my duty?"

"You have, and I thank you."

"Don't thank me." He tapped my shoulder with one of his sausage-sized fingers. "Do me a favor. Tell folks what a good citizen Gus Peppermill is, how Gus Peppermill came all the way back from Glen Ellen in his fixit wagon to give you important information."

I smiled a little. "Free advertising, eh?"

"And why not? I do good work—people know that. Can't hurt if they also knew the fixit man is a good citizen."

"All right, Gus. I'll spread the word."

He nodded cheerfully and climbed back into his wagon. And I went looking for Morton Brandeis.

CHAPTER 7

HE wasn't at home. His wife's sister, Maude Seeley, who had moved in to care for Lucy when she took sick, told me she thought Morton had gone down to the livery. But he was not there either. Jacob Pike—without looking me in the eye, polite as can be—said that Sam McCullough had stopped by a few minutes earlier and Morton had gone with him over to the saddlery. That was Pike for you: snotty and troublesome until he sensed he had pushed you too far, then quiet and toadyish, as though butter wouldn't melt in his mouth. No backbone. And a good thing, too, or he would probably have got into serious trouble sooner or later.

I went to the saddlery. Morton was there, giving Sam advice on some tooling he wanted done on the gullet and fork of an old California saddle he had bought from the estate of a Chileno Valley cowman. Sam was restoring the saddle for him.

I asked Morton to step outside with me, led him over into the shade of a pepper tree. From there you could see the black oak out back where Jeremy Bodeen had been hanged. I did not like looking at it and I put my backside to it as we talked.

"Gus Peppermill's back in town," I said.

"Is he? How come?"

I told him how come. "Gus says he passed you not long after Jeremy Bodeen, coming from out Stage

Gulch way. Says you were riding fast and Bodeen was just ambling."

"Last Tuesday?"

"Same day Bodeen was hanged."

Morton dragged out his pipe and tobacco pouch and began loading up. There was a set look to his face, as if he were working his memory. "Oh, sure," he said at length. "That was the day I went to see Ben Cohoon about a couple of horses he had for sale. Buckskin and a strawberry roan. But his price was too high—"

"Never mind that, Morton. It's Jeremy Bodeen I'm interested in. You must have seen him; why didn't you tell me about it?"

"I don't recall seeing him, Linc. I don't."

"Man heading the same way you were, a stranger, and you likely passed him and didn't even notice?"

"I . . . had things on my mind."

"Mind saying what they were?"

"Personal things. You know Lucy's condition."

"Yes," I said. "How is she?"

"Poorly." There was something in his face now that I could not quite read. He struck a lucifer, waved away the sulphur, and then fired his tobacco. "Wish I could help you, Linc. But I just don't recall seeing Bodeen."

At the livery again I told Jacob Pike to saddle my horse, a chalk-eye pinto I had bought off Charley Casebeer out at Two Rock last year. I called him Rowdy—the horse, not Charley Casebeer—because he was warm-blooded, liked to run, and kept fretting at the snaffle whenever I held him back. He had thrown me twice, once into a patch of nettles, but you had to expect that kind of behavior with a dauncy horse. I liked his spirit.

I rode out of town to the east, toward the Sonoma

Mountains. Once we were into open countryside, I gave
Rowdy his head and let him frisk along for a while. I
had not ridden in days and it was good to be in the
saddle again.

It was three miles to Willow Creek Road, and another
two along there to the Parsons' tenant farm. There were
a few cattle and sheep ranches out this way, but most of
the land this side of Stage Gulch was agricultural—
alfalfa and barley and other crops—broken up by half
a dozen creeks and stands of native trees and rows of
those Australian imports, eucalpytus, that lose their
bark once a year in great peeling strips; some farmers
and ranchers had taken to them because they grew fast
and made good windbreaks. The day was warm but the
air had that rich fall smell that tells you the season is
about to change again and winter is nigh: a mixture of
things dead and dying, and new growths getting ready
to sprout in their places once the rains came.

A rutted trail hooked up to the Parsons farm from
Willow Creek Road. The acreage was modest—just a
few fields of corn and alfalfa, with a cluster of buildings
set near where Willow Creek cut through the northwest
corner. There was a one-room farmhouse, a cookshack,
a chicken pen, a barn, a couple of lean-tos, and a pole
corral. That was all except for a small windmill—a
Fairbanks, Morse Eclipse—that the Siler brothers, who
lived over near Sonoma, had put up because the creek
was dry more than half the year.

When I came in sight of the buildings I could see that
Jubal Parsons had done work on the place. The previous
tenants had let it run down some; now the farmhouse
had a fresh coat of whitewash, as did the chicken coop,
and the fences had been mended and the barn had a
new roof.

There was nobody in the farmyard, just a couple of foraging roosters, when I rode in. Quiet here; the rattle and squeak of the windmill blades and an occasional squawk from the leghorns in their pens were the only sounds.

Smoke was pouring out through the cookhouse chimney, so I got down in front of the main house and tied Rowdy to the porch rail and then walked around to the cookhouse. The door was open and Greta Parsons was sitting on a bench inside, peeling thin strips from a block of wax and letting them drop into a clay bowl in her lap. Alongside her was a brass candle mold, and on an old soot-black stove at the far end, a pair of kettles were heating.

She heard me and looked up, squinting. She knew her husband's step and the angle of the sun must have been wrong for her to see me clearly, for she called out, "Who's that?"

"It's Lincoln Evans, Mrs. Parsons." I came ahead into the doorway, taking off my hat. "Didn't startle you, did I?"

"No. We don't have many visitors."

"Well, I hope you don't mind my dropping in on the Sabbath this way. ... ."

"The Sabbath is just another workday for us."

It was warm in the sun but even warmer inside the cookhouse, with the fire going in the stove. The air was thick with the smells of hot wax and a familiar spiciness.

"Bayberry," I said, sniffing. "Always was partial to bayberry candles." I did not add that Ivy wasn't partial to them and so they were never burned in our house.

"I like them too. They are better made with sheep tallow but I didn't have enough."

"Wax is about as good," I said. "My ma used to make

her bayberry candles that way. Shavings so the wax melts quick in hot water without burning. Scoop the grease off when it comes to the top, then strain it through cheesecloth and pour it into the molds. That right?"

"Yes. I made several yesterday—would you like one?"

"Well, as a matter of fact, I would." I was thinking that I could burn it in my office. "I'll be glad to pay for it. . . ."

"That isn't necessary. We have plenty. What brings you way out here, Mr. Evans?"

"Just a few questions I'd like to ask you and your husband."

"Questions?"

"Is he within hailing distance? I didn't see him anywhere when I rode in."

"I believe he's mending fence." She set the bowl and knife and block of wax next to the mold and got to her feet. "I'll show you where."

I backed up and she came out into the sunlight. She cut a fine figure even in a plain muslin dress. That butter-yellow hair of hers was pinned up in braids but little strands had worked their way loose and poked out here and there, like bright feathers. She fussed with one of them that had strayed down onto the bridge of her nose. In the sunbright, the hardness that marred her features and her eyes made her seem less attractive than she had in the gloom of the cookhouse. No less desirable, though.

We went along to the front of the main house, and she pointed toward a low hill to the west. "You'll find Jubal somewhere over that hill yonder," she said. "At least, that was where he said he was going after our noon meal."

"Will you answer a few questions yourself?"

"If I can. What is it you want to know?"

"Well, it's about the man who was murdered in town last week. Jeremy Bodeen. You heard about that when you were in the other day?"

A frown wrinkled the sun-dark skin of her forehead. "Yes, we heard. But we know nothing about it. Why would you think we do?"

"I don't think it," I said. "I'm here because Gus Peppermill, the fixit man, passed Bodeen on Willow Creek Road around four last Tuesday afternoon, the same day he was killed."

"Yes?"

"Gus said there was a farm wagon on the road behind him at the time, and that Bodeen passed it as it was about to turn in at your gate. He said the driver was a woman. You, Mrs. Parsons?"

"Yes. I recall seeing the fixit wagon on the road ahead of me when I drove out at the creek fork. I go there sometimes to pick watercress. Best place around for it."

"You remember seeing Bodeen too?"

"A man on horseback, yes. But I had no idea that is who he was."

"He say anything to you?"

"He did not."

"Just rode on by without stopping?"

"I don't know if he stopped. I didn't look back; I had no reason to."

"Did you see him again, by any chance?"

"No. Only that once, at a glance. I couldn't even tell you what he looked like."

"Could your husband have seen him?"

"I don't see how he could have," she said. "He was here, working in the chicken pen, when I arrived."

"Well, I'll ask him anyhow."

"I'm sorry I can't be of more help, Mr. Evans. If you'll wait just a minute, I'll get that bayberry candle for you."

She went into the house. Directly she reappeared with a fat white candle twice the size of the ones she had been molding in the cookshack earlier. "It's one of my Christmas candles," she said, handing it to me. "You might want to keep it until the holidays."

"I'll do that. Thank you kindly."

"Not at all."

I swung up onto Rowdy's back, put the candle into the saddle pouch. Mrs. Parsons gave me a brief smile and then turned back toward the cookhouse. She walked straight as a stick, with her head up high—proud, the way Hannah walked.

I reined away from the house and rode up to the crest of the low hill. On the far side, near a clutch of live oaks, a man in his undershirt was working on a section of line fence. To one side of him was the Parsons' farm wagon, a ploddy-looking gray in the trace and some tools and sharpened fence posts in the bed. To the other side was a spool of new barbed wire, one strand of it trailing along the ground like a spiky silver thread.

He heard me coming when I was halfway downslope, straightened around and stood stiff-backed and unmoving as I neared him. He was a tall, spare man, dark, with bushy hair cut high above the ears and neck. No more than thirty-five, I judged, but there was something austere about him that made him seem much older.

"Afternoon, Mr. Parsons."

"Constable Evans."

"Talk to you a while?"

"I've more fence to mend before dark."

"I won't take up much of your time."

He watched me as I dismounted. His face was as dark

and webbed as sun-cured leather, and it made his deep-set eyes look even darker than they were—as black and shiny as brine-soaked olives. He had a pair of wire-cutters in one gloved hand, and he kept snicking the blades together; the squeezing movement caused the corded sinews along his arm to writhe and ripple, like snakes under a blanket.

He said, "How did you know where to find me?"

"I just spoke to your wife."

"I see."

"Fine woman," I said. "She gave me one of her bay-berry Christmas candles."

"For what reason?"

"No reason. Neighborly gesture, that's all."

He made a grunting sound, as if he did not approve of neighborly gestures. "What is it you want of me, Mr. Evans?"

"Some questions about Jeremy Bodeen."

"I know no one named Jeremy Bodeen."

"The man who was found hanged in Tule Bend last week," I said. "Name Bodeen isn't familiar to you?"

"No."

"His brother's in town. Emmett Bodeen."

"That is no business of mine."

Disagreeable cuss, I thought. I told him about Gus Peppermill seeing Jeremy Bodeen on Willow Creek Road, and about Mrs. Parsons being there at the same time. For all the expression on his face, I might have been telling him a dull story he had heard a dozen times before.

When I was done talking, he said, "My wife said nothing about it to me."

"Wasn't worth mentioning, I guess. She didn't connect

the rider she saw with Bodeen. Didn't speak to him, she said."

"My wife is not in the habit of speaking to passing strangers."

"I didn't suppose she was. You didn't happen to see the man yourself, did you?"

"I did not."

"Nor at any other time last Tuesday?"

"I was here all of last Tuesday."

"Didn't leave the farm all day?"

"I did not," Parsons said.

"Well, then."

"Is that the last of your questions, Mr. Evans?"

"It is. I'll leave you to your work."

He dipped his chin at me, then turned and bent in one motion and snipped off the trailing length of barbed wire from the spool. As far as he was concerned, I was already gone.

I put Rowdy under me again and rode up to the brow of the hill. When I looked back from there, Parsons was hammering a staple into one of the new fence posts to secure the length of wire. Putting muscle into the job, too; the whacks of his hammer were like pistol shots in the still air.

Strange man, as well as a disagreeable one. I found myself wondering, as I rode on past the farm buildings, why a woman like Greta Parsons had married him; what she had seen in him that had attracted her. Whatever it was, it was beyond my powers of reckoning. And none of my concern, either. For all they seemed oddly mated, they might be happy and content together. You can't tell about a married couple. You would have to be one of a particular pair to understand the way things were between them, and even then you might not be too certain on some counts.

Still and all, I could not help thinking that she didn't *look* happy and content. And that maybe she deserved better than this tenant farm and better than Jubal Parsons.

CHAPTER 8

SEEING Greta Parsons that afternoon made me want to
see Hannah that night, I suppose partly because of the
similarities between them. I thought about Hannah all
the way back to town, and off and on during the afternoon, and while I endured Ivy's pry-and-prattle over
supper. Soon after we finished eating I got my coat and
went out and walked around on the east side of town
for a while, letting enough time pass so that I would not
interrupt Hannah's supper and any evening chores she
might have. It was near nine when I finally walked back
across the bridge and through town and climbed the
rise to the Dalton house.

Hannah was on the porch, as usual, and again I had
the notion she was pleased to see me. I also thought I
detected a measure of concern in her voice when she
asked, "How are you feeling, Lincoln?" right after she
let me in.

"Feeling?"

"Your head. The prowler last night."

"You know about that?" I asked, surprised.

"Oh yes. All about it."

"How? I didn't see you in town today. . . ."

"I wasn't in town today."

"But I thought that—"

"That I didn't have callers? I don't, usually." She
smiled. It was difficult to tell in the lamplight, but there
did not seem to be any humor in it. "The good citizens

71

of Tule Bend tell me things on occasion," she said. "Things they want me to know."

"I don't understand."

"Does it really matter, Lincoln?"

"It does to me. Why would somebody want you to know I was hurt last night?"

"You're sitting here with me now, aren't you?"

"You mean because I come here to see you?"

"At night. You come at night."

"Hannah, I . . ."

"The whole town knows about it," she said. "Did you think it was a secret?"

"No. And I don't care what the town knows."

"The town cares," she said.

"To hell with the town."

"You don't mean that."

"I do mean it. By God, I do. It's nobody's business but yours and mine."

"You're naive if you believe that. The town constable keeping company with the town whore—that is everyone's business, like it or not."

Heat had come into my face. I leaned toward her. "What kind of talk is that? You're not a . . . you're not that kind of woman."

"The town thinks I am."

"Damn the town!"

"Don't shout, Lincoln. Please."

I *had* shouted, the first time I had ever raised my voice to her. It shamed me; she was the victim, not the villain, and I had no right to be railing at her in any case. I sat back in my chair, put a tight rein on my feelings before I asked, soft, "Who was it told you about my trouble with the prowler?"

"I'd rather not say."

"I'd rather you did. I want to know."

"Why? So you can confront the person?"

"I just want to know."

"It isn't important," Hannah said. "If I give you one name, I might as well give you half a dozen. People are the way they are—you must know that. You can't change them; no one can change them except themselves, and most have no desire to change."

"That doesn't mean I have to accept it."

"But you do. You *do* accept it."

"I don't."

"You live here, you're part of the town. We both are. As long as we choose to remain, you and I must accept what people say and think about us, what they believe we are."

To have something to do with my hands, I got out my pipe and tamped tobacco into the bowl. I did not say anything.

"Lincoln? You know I'm right."

"Maybe so. But I don't have to like it."

When she spoke again there was an edge of strain to the words. "I've coffee made. Or would you rather go?" Leaving it up to me.

I didn't hesitate. "I'd like to stay, if you'll allow it."

"Of course."

She touched my arm, let her hand linger for a second—the first time she had ever touched me with any intimacy. Then she stood and entered the house.

I sat quiet, fancying that I could still feel the heat of her fingers. There was a dull ache down low in my belly—an ache I knew too well, that in the past had led me down to one of the parlor houses in San Francisco when it became too much to tolerate. But at the same time I felt uneasy and confused and not a little angry.

People coming up here on some pretext or other, telling Hannah things about me, making their snide comments to her and to each other—and there wasn't a thing I could do about it. *People are the way they are . . . you can't change them . . . as long as we remain here, you and I must accept what people say and think about us. . . .*

Crockery rattled inside, a different sound than when Ivy rattled it at home—or maybe that was just fancy too. The moon was up and it put a silver tint on the rolling wooded hills to the east, painted a stripe of silver on the black path of the creek. Farther south, dredger lights winked and a flat-bottomed boat with a lantern on a pole drifted around a bend toward the S.F. & N.P. swing bridge. A nightbird cried out somewhere, low and trembly, like a lament for something or somebody that had died.

Hannah came back with her coffee service and set the tray on the table between us. When she leaned over to pour, the lampglow showed me the curve of her breast and hips and I smelled again the sweet scent of her sachet. That low-down ache sharpened. What would she do if I touched her, tried to kiss her? Yield, or slap my face and order me to leave?

You're not a . . . you're not that kind of woman.

The town thinks I am.

Damn the town!

I looked away from her, scraped my mind clear of carnal thoughts, and worked at lighting my pipe. But it was not lust. Ivy would have called it lust, the bluenoses in Tule Bend would have, but it was more than that, it was purer than that . . . damn the town. Goddamn the town!

Neither of us spoke for a time. The silence was better now, easier. I drank the chickory-flavored coffee and smoked my pipe and watched the night. And glanced at Hannah every now and then, when it got to be too much of an effort to hold my eyes away.

I was looking at her when she said, "Have you found out anything more about the man who was hanged?"

"No," I said. "Not much."

"You will."

"So I keep telling myself and everyone else."

"Don't you believe it?"

"I'm worried, Hannah, I don't mind telling you that."

"Why?"

"Because I haven't found out more than I have— that's one thing. Another is Emmett Bodeen, the dead man's brother; he's a troublemaker, for sure. Then there was that prowler last night. Too much has happened too fast and it makes me edgy."

"You think there'll be more trouble?"

"Yes," I said, "I do. I can feel it."

And I could, too, the way you can feel a storm building long before it breaks. More trouble was coming, all right. I was prepared for it.

What I was not prepared for was how fast it arrived.

CHAPTER 9

THERE was a bell ringing somewhere, a long way off.

It got mixed up with the already muddled dream I was having, then brought me groggily awake. Pitch black in my bedroom—middle of the night? And that distant clamor kept on and on. . . .

Fire bell.

The realization woke me up good and proper. Our fire bell used to hang in the belfry of the old Methodist church on Tule Bend Road, before the congregation raised the money a few years back to build a new church. When the old one was torn down, the bell was donated to the town and mounted on the wall of the Volunteer Fire Brigade on Main. It had a crack in it, like the Liberty Bell, so there was no mistaking its sound. And when it pealed as it was pealing now, loud and steady with no pauses, it meant a big blaze somewhere within the town limits—a major alarm.

I swung out of bed, managed to get to the window without falling over anything in the dark. The window faced north and when I raised the shade, there was nothing to see out that way except a faint reddish tinge. The fire was somewhere on the south side of town, then, or west or east. I turned back to the bed and groped for my clothes and got my trousers and boots on standing up. All the while that fire bell kept hammering out its urgent summons.

I put my shirt and coat on over my nightshirt, not

buttoning either one, and stumbled out into the hall. Ivy was coming from the direction of her room, carrying a lighted lamp; in her long white nightdress, her pale face backlit by the lamplight, she looked like a scrawny apparition—one of those female ghosts that are supposed to haunt manor houses over in England.

"Mercy sakes, Lincoln, mercy sakes." Her voice was all a-quiver. But there was as much thrill in it as there was concern, like a tent show preacher's in the throes of a sermon about sins of the flesh. "What is it? What could have caught fire at three o'clock in the morning?"

Foolish questions, so I didn't bother to answer. I ran down the stairs, onto the front porch. Outside the racket from the bell built echo after echo until the night itself seemed to have come alive. I could see lights flare up in the other houses along the block, people starting to spill out through open doorways; I could see the blaze, too, or rather the smoke and the weird pulsing glow lighting up the sky, and it dried my mouth, put a tightness in my chest. Whatever was burning was on this side of the creek, smack downtown.

"Oh my Lord!" Ivy, behind me at the door. "It . . . why, half the town must be on fire!"

I had no answer for that, either.

My bicycle was at the Odd Fellows Hall, so I jumped off the porch and ran toward Main, buttoning up the rest of my clothing as I went. Others joined me along the way, one of them Sam McCullough. Under the pealing clamor of the fire bell, voices lifted in shouts of consternation and bewilderment.

Trees and houses obscured my view until I reached Main. Then I could see what it was: two buildings in the third business block, just which ones I couldn't tell yet, both sheeted with flame. Burning hot and fast, the way salt-weathered wood structures will. Sparks and embers flecked the smoke that roiled up into the night sky— and there was just enough wind to carry them to nearby buildings, most of which were also old and made of wood. If the wind picked up any more, the whole block was liable to go up like dry tinder in a stove. I had seen it happen once before in Tule Bend, across the creek near the S.F. & N.P. yards seven years ago; six buildings and two men had died in that conflagration. This one could be much worse. If the fire spread to Far West Milling and Beecher's Lumberyard and Creekside Dray-age, it would burn the heart right out of Tule Bend.

"Christ, that's *my* place!"

Sam McCullough, running a few paces ahead of me. His saddlery shop, all right. And the second pyre was Joel Pennywell's carpentry shop next door.

Sam broke stride, gawking in disbelief. I ran past him without slowing. There was nothing I could say to him now, and no time to say it if there had been.

The firehouse was in the next block north of the two burning buildings. By the time I reached it, half a dozen men had the hose and pump carts out and were drag-ging them, axles squealing, across the street toward the creek. Firelight bathed the street in a ruddy glow that glinted off window glass, made blackened silhouettes of the running, milling citizens.

The man working the fire bell was George Brady, the night operator at the Western Union office. I yelled to him, "What happened, George?"

"Ask Walt Barber if you can find him," he shouted back. "He's the one came and got me. Said he saw somebody running away from Sam's place just after it blazed up."

"The hell he did! Who?"

"Said he didn't get a good look."

Walt Barber was the closest Tule Bend had to a town drunk. He lived in a shack downstream, did odd jobs and ranchwork, drank up most of what he earned. But I had never seen him falling-down drunk, never had to arrest him for public intoxication or any other offense. Harmless fellow, had most of his wits about him even when he was liquored up. If he had told George Brady that he had seen a man running away from the saddlery, then it was a good bet he had. . . .

No time to fret over it now. Or to go hunting for Walt Barber. That fire was getting hotter; I could feel the heat even this far away, hear it thrumming and crackling as it licked up and around at the dark. Embers danced out of the flame-edged smoke . . . and an exploded pine knot as big as a baseball that narrowly missed landing on the tar-paper roof of Kelliher's grocery. If Kelliher's went up, the next three buildings bunched close on its north side would go too—and fast, like torched haystacks. Then only the narrow expanse of Sonoma Street would separate the blaze from Far West Milling and the other buildings lining the basin on this side.

I raced across the street, past the north wall of the grocery. A score of men were already working along the creekbank, some unwinding and laying out fifty-foot lengths of fire hose and coupling them together, others working with the pumps. I cut over to the nearest pump to lend a hand.

One of the men there was Bert Lawless, the volunteer fire chief. He was also Tule Bend's champion complainer, even at a time like this. He said as I came up, "Goddamn pump don't want to work right. I told Gladstone and the council we needed new equipment, goddamn it I *told* them. . . ."

A sharp sucking noise came from the pump's intake and shut him up. Somebody else said unnecessarily, "She's working now, Bert."

"About the goddamn time."

I said. "We've got to get Kelliher's soaked down first thing, stop any spread toward the basin."

"Don't tell me how to fight a fire, Linc," Lawless said in his cantankerous way. "I *know* what we got to do first thing."

"Then let's do it."

I helped carry the heavy brass nozzle up the bank and over to the grocery, while other volunteers laid the hose out in a line behind to lessen weight and side-pull once the water started to flow. When we were ready I signaled back for them to start the pump again. The hose and nozzle bucked like a dauncy horse; it took three of us to keep the stream of water aimed and steady.

Kelliher's tar-paper roof was smouldering in two places toward the back. We managed to douse both spots in time to keep the entire roof from catching. Then we drenched the rest of it, and the side wall nearest the saddlery. The heat from the flames was tremendous. Sweat rolled off me in rivulets; the back of my neck felt raw. Once, a piece of burning wood landed on my shoulder and scorched a hole through my coat before I could slap it off.

We were moving around to the front when the pump pressure suddenly fell and the stream of water slackened to a pizzle spurt. Lawless said, "Goddamnit, now what?"

Letting the others have the hose, Lawless and I ran back to the creek to see what the trouble was. Mud clogging the intake hose. By the time we helped clear it, the hardware store on the south side of Joel Pennywell's caught fire. I let Lawless go back alone to continue the work on Kelliher's, and joined one of the hose crews working at the hardware store.

Just as it seemed we were winning the battle there, the carpentry shop's roof collapsed in a thunderous roar and a geysering fountain of sparks and embers. One of the volunteers was struck by a flying section of roof beam and knocked flat; I saw that, and I saw his clothing begin to smoulder as he struggled to free himself. The beam had fallen across one of his legs and had him pinned.

I got to him within a few seconds. It was Sam Mc-Cullough—as if this night had not been enough of a disaster for him already. Dragging my coat off, I kicked at the beam fragment—I did not dare touch it with my bare hands—and sent it rolling off his leg. Then I dropped down beside him, smothered the burning cloth of his trousers. The inferno's smoke and searing heat robbed both of us of breath, had us choking and me half blind by the time others reached us and pulled us away.

I had to sit for a couple of minutes, back across Main, until my eyes and lungs cleared; but I was sound enough otherwise. Sam had not been so lucky. He had burns on both legs and maybe a couple of cracked ribs. Two of the men carried him over to the firehouse, where Doc Petersen and several women had set up a first-aid station.

Helpless and angry, I sat watching the fires pulse out smoke and throw quivery goblin shadows across the faces of the scurrying volunteers; listening to the heat-crackle, the snapping of timbers, the hiss and spit of water pouring out of the hoses, the shouts and cries and curses. It was like a glimpse of the Pit, and it seemed to go on and on.

The hardware store was burning now too. Forks of flame had claimed one wall and part of its roof. Dry grass in lots on its south side and across the street had also been touched off. When I was ready and able I went back to join the hose crew working there. We extinguished the grass fires before any more buildings were threatened, but there was nothing anybody could do to save the hardware store. Before long it, too, was an inferno.

There were more tense minutes when the saddlery's roof collapsed. But a proper job had been done of soaking down Kelliher's, so the grocery did not catch and there was no spread of the fire in that direction. When the wind began to die down instead of gusting I finally let myself believe we would be able to confine the damage to the lower half of this one block; that we had the fire tamed and close to being licked.

It was another hour, though, and dawnlight was seeping into the eastern sky, before it was completely under control. The final tally was three buildings lost; smoke, fire, and water damage to three others; a few injuries, most of them minor, and no loss of life. Bad enough, but not nearly as bad as it might have been, thanks to the combined efforts of just about every able-bodied man in Tule Bend.

I was exhausted, smoke-grimed and heat-seared, but my work for the night was not done yet. I took a couple of minutes, down at the creek, to wash my hands and douse my head with icy water. Boze was one of a knot of others nearby; I called him over, related what George Brady had told me, and together we went looking for Walt Barber.

It didn't take us long to find him. He was at the firehouse, drinking a dipperful of fresh water from a tub some of the women had brought and filled. Judging from the look of him, he had been on the fire lines too; his lean, scarecrow shape was almost as sooty as Boze's and mine. He was also cold sober, and a little on the shaky side because of it.

We took him aside and I asked him about the man he had seen running away from the saddlery. He said, "I didn't see him up close, Mr. Evans. But from a ways off . . . well, I don't believe he's anybody I know."

"You sure he came out of the saddlery?"

"Well, I didn't see him come out. But he was nearby."

"Which did you see first, him or the fire?"

"Fire. I was just about to run and tell Mr. Brady about it when he come runnin' out of the shadders."

"Where were you at the time?"

"Down toward the creekbank. On my way home."

"Which direction did he go?"

"South. I don't think he seen me."

"How long did you watch after him?"

"Few seconds. I think he was headed for the livery."

"All right. Can you tell us anything that might identify him? How big he was, what he was wearing—whatever you can remember about him."

"Well," Walt said, "well, he wasn't big and he wasn't small. Wore dark clothes." I watched him squinch up his eyes while he worked his memory. "Had long hair . . . yes, sir, long hair. I seen it flyin' out when he was runnin'."

"What color hair?"

"Dark. Black, I reckon. Like a Inyan."

There was a sharpness in my next question: "What about facial hair, Walt? Mustache, beard?"

"Mustache," he said immediately. "I seen it plain."

"Big thick one?"

"Yes, sir. Big thick one."

I fished around in my trouser pocket, found a silver cartwheel, and pressed it into Walt's shaky hand. He blinked at me and said, "You don't need to give me nothing, Mr. Evans. . . ."

"I know it. But you've earned a drink, Walt. Go find yourself one."

I nudged Boze, and as we started away he said, "You thinkin' what I'm thinkin'?"

"Emmett Bodeen," I said.

"But why? Don't make sense he'd want to burn up Sam McCullough's saddle shop."

"Maybe it does. His brother was hanged right out back of Sam's, remember. Might even have been in his mind to destroy the whole town."

"What the devil for?"

"Warped kind of justice for his brother."

"You mean he blames all of *us?* Hell, Linc . . ."

"Crazier things have happened. And he has been on a short fuse ever since he came here."

"Yeah." Boze still had a touch of the grippe; he snuffled, blew drip in that unsanitary way of his, and snuffled again. "You figure Bodeen was the prowler you tangled with last night?" he asked.

"Can't say yet. But it's likely. His first idea could have been to set fire to the livery."

"Well, he's long gone by now, that's for sure," Boze said. "Only one reason for him to head for the livery tonight—get that old roan horse of his brother's so he could make tracks out of town."

I nodded. "We'll see if the roan's gone. If it is, we'll

put out a fugitive warrant. Not much else we can do, now; he's had a good three hours' head start."

We had been moving downstreet, away from the smoldering remains of the three buildings and the citizens who had not yet begun to straggle homeward. Ahead, the livery barn loomed dark against the pink-gray sky. No lights showed anywhere.

The front doors were secure, so we went on around to the rear. There were streamers of mist on the creek now, an early-morning chill in the air, a layer of frost on the grass; the coldness was like a balm on my burnt face. Or it was until I saw that the rear doors were standing wide open and nobody was around. Then I felt the chill in a different way: gooseflesh rippling along the saddle of my back.

"Now that's funny," Boze said. "Doors wide open like that, half the horses could have run off by now. Why the hell wouldn't Pike . . . ?"

I said, "You see him anywhere back at the fire?"

"No. Kid like that wouldn't risk *his* hide on a fire line."

I thought the same. Which meant that Pike had probably been here when Bodeen showed up.

I moved ahead to the open doors and called out, "Jacob! Jacob Pike!"

An echo of my voice and then silence.

I went inside by a few paces, squinting into the gloom. On the runway not far ahead, a manure cart lay on its side as if it had been kicked over by a horse—or a man. Most of the animals looked to have remained in their stalls. But one stall that *was* empty, I saw, was the one that had been occupied by Jeremy Bodeen's swaybacked roan.

At my elbow Boze said, "Want me to have a look up in the loft?"

"Yes. I'll check the tack room."

He went ahead to the loft ladder and I turned toward the harness room on my right, breathing through my mouth now because the ammoniac stable smell seemed stronger than usual this morning. Or perhaps it was just that my senses had been sharpened by the fire, by the look and feel of the barn.

I was just opening the harness room door when Boze shouted, "Linc! Christ Almighty—Linc!"

He was over next to the loft ladder, staring at something I couldn't see because of the angle of the tack room wall. I ran to his side. And when I did see what he was looking at, the cold on my back deepened and sent out shivers.

Jacob Pike was back there in the shadows. Suspended from a rafter beam, his head flopped over on one side, his eyes wide and bulging, his tongue poked out at one corner of his mouth.

Hanged just like Jeremy Bodeen.

CHAPTER 10

WE stood looking up at the body for several seconds, neither of us moving. But it seemed that Pike was swaying a little up there in the shadows, at the end of that stretched-taut rope—a draft, maybe, or just my fancy. I thought I could hear the rope creak, too, like a devil's whisper. I felt another shiver ripple my back, and when Boze turned away I did the same.

He said thickly, "Kid like Pike . . . why would Bodeen do that to him?"

"If it was Bodeen."

"Who the hell else?"

I shook my head.

"Must have been Bodeen," Boze said. "Maybe he thought Pike had something to do with hangin' his brother."

Shook my head again.

"You want me to go fetch Doc Petersen?" he asked after a few seconds.

"Yes. Tell him what happened here but don't tell anybody else. Town will find out soon enough and I don't want anyone blundering around and getting in the way."

"Right."

"Another thing," I said. "On your way, stop at the office and pick up my change of clothes and a handgun and rigging. That Bisley Colt of mine. And wrap it in the clothing so you're not seen toting it."

"How come you want all that?"

"Just get moving. We'll talk about it when you come back."

I followed him to the rear doors, took the lantern there down from its wall peg, lighted it after Boze was gone, and then closed myself inside. The first thing I did was to have a look at the horses. My chalk-eye was still in his stall; Jeremy Bodeen's roan was definitely missing. Possible that it had run off, but more likely it had been ridden away by Emmett Bodeen. I could not tell which other animals might be gone, or whose they might be.

I carried the lantern back to the overturned manure cart. It wasn't the only indication that there had been a struggle here. There were scuff marks in the hard sod of the runway—the kind made by boot heels and toes— and a board in one of the grain bins was cracked, as though somebody had been flung hard against it. I walked around there with the lantern down close to the ground. At the base of another bin, something glinted in the light. I sat on my heels and picked it up.

A circlet of bronze, about three inches in diameter. When I held it close to the light I saw that it was one of those presidential medals the government issued a few years back at the Philadelphia Mint. On one side it bore a likeness of Benjamin Harrison, along with his name and the date of his inauguration, 1889; on the other were a tomahawk, a peace pipe, and a pair of clasped hands.

There weren't many such medals in California; mostly they had been supplied to army officers in other parts of the West, who handed them out to Indians after peace treaties were signed. I had seen one on display in

San Francisco once, but I had never seen one in Tule Bend until now.

I put the medal into my pocket, hunted around a while longer without finding anything else, then climbed the ladder to the loft. Jacob Pike's living quarters were at the rear—an eight-foot square "room" formed by the front and side walls of the barn, with the other two walls being chest-high slabs of plywood nailed to two-by-four frames. Inside were a straw bunk, an ironbound trunk, a small homemade table, and a sheet-metal heating stove with a pipe running out through the side wall. The floor had been swept clean of straw, not so much because Pike was tidy, I thought, as a precaution against fire.

The trunk contained Pike's meager possessions: a couple of changes of clothing, the two halves of a professional pool cue wrapped in chamois, a Merwin & Hulbert five-shot .38 single-action with the firing pin gone, a book called *Snappy Jokes*, a celluloid button that said "Oh Honey Give Me Some" on it, and half a dozen obscene French postcards that I would have liked, perversely, to have taken home and showed to Ivy just to hear her scream. That was all. Nothing there to tie Pike to the murder of Jeremy Bodeen, or to make him a likely candidate for a lynching. And it did not look as though the trunk had been searched by anyone before me, as though anything might be missing from it.

I looked under the bunk and poked around the straw tick, even opened the door to the stove and used a stick propped nearby to stir among the ashes. Nothing. Finally I climbed back down to the runway and made myself take another look at Pike hanging up there in the gloom.

What had happened here tonight? Pike must have

been wakened by the fire bell, I thought, and put his clothes on—his corpse was fully dressed—and come down to see what was going on. When he unbarred the doors he was jumped, and there was a fight, and Pike lost it and then lost his life. That much seemed fairly clear. But what was not clear was who had killed him and why.

Two possibilities, I thought, and neither of them seemed to make much sense. If it was Emmett Bodeen who had strung him up like that, it had to be because Bodeen thought Pike was mixed up in the killing of his brother. Only I couldn't see Pike committing a cold-blooded homicide by lynching. It took a certain kind of courage to kill a man, and a crazy, vicious, cunning streak to do it by hanging smack in the middle of town. Pike had been a coward, and a slow-witted one at that. Had he witnessed Jeremy Bodeen's murder, then, or known something about it? Maybe. But then why would Emmett Bodeen have killed him? I could picture Bodeen putting a rope around a man's neck to avenge his brother, but I could not see him doing it to anyone but the actual murderer.

The other possibility was that the same man had done both killings. And that worried me the most, because likely it meant there was a madman on the loose in Tule Bend after all. Who else but a madman would want to hang a drifter and a stablehand? There was just no rational motive in either case. Pike had not been liked much but I couldn't imagine anyone having a killing grudge against him. Random victim, then, same as Jeremy Bodeen? Two men in the wrong place at the wrong time, victims of somebody's bloodlust?

And yet . . .

I kept remembering the prowler who had clubbed me

on Saturday night. Two different prowlers at a livery barn on successive nights was a hell of a coincidence. What if the one last night *hadn't* been after a horse or a place to start a fire? What if he had been after Jacob Pike? And what if he had come back tonight to do the job he'd planned on his first visit?

Well, that put me right back to my starting place. Who would want to kill Pike and why? Had the same person who did for him started the fire, maybe as a diversion? And if it was not Emmett Bodeen, then had Bodeen seen Pike's murderer before he lit a shuck for parts unknown?

All the questions and confused possibilities were making my head hurt. I was having trouble keeping my thoughts straight anyway, as fatigued as I was from the fire fight. What I needed was sleep. But the way things were now, I was not likely to get any for some time to come.

I set to work untying the end of the hangrope from where it had been looped around a stall post. It was knotted tight but I managed to work the knot loose without having to cut it. I was just lowering Pike's corpse to the ground when Boze returned with Doc Petersen.

Doc was wearing his nightshirt under his greatcoat and he looked as weary as I felt from his ministerings at the fire. He was grumpy, too. He said irascibly, "I was just getting ready for bed. Didn't even have time to close my eyes." Then he took a long look at the body, and there was a different tone to his voice when he said, "What in hell's going on in this town, Linc?"

"I wish I knew."

"You had better find out soon, my boy. Once news of this gets out, there's liable to be a panic. You know what I'm talking about."

I knew, all right. Folks arming themselves and carrying their weapons openly, mistrusting every stranger
and before long friends and neighbors as well, maybe
shooting at shadows, then maybe shooting at each other.
The longer the fear and uncertainty were allowed to
fester, the uglier things would get—to the point of
martial law being declared. And if it did get to that
point, more citizens would likely die . . . and not by the
hand of a madman, either.

Doc picked up the lantern I had set down, carried it
over to where Pike lay. He went to one knee to peer at
the body, his back to Boze and me. Boze touched my
arm and motioned with his head that he wanted to talk
in private. We went over by the grain bins, out of Doc's
earshot.

He had my Bisley Colt and its holster and cartridge
belt wrapped in the change of clothes I keep in the
office for emergencies; he handed the bundle to me as
he spoke. "Just keeps gettin' worse, Linc. I didn't tell
Doc because I didn't want to get him any more riled
than he is, but I ran into Fred Horler on the way to
Doc's house. He was lookin' for you and fit to be tied.
Verne Gladstone was with him."

"Now what?"

"Somebody busted into Fred's office at Far West and
made off with his cashbox. He had more in it than
usual, on account of today being payday. Six hundred
dollars."

"Christ!"

"More of Bodeen's handiwork—the son of a bitch."

"You didn't tell Fred and the mayor about Pike?"

"No. They'd have been all over you by now if I had."

"Good. You'll have to tell them eventually, though."

"Why me?"

"I won't be here, that's why. I'll be out hunting Bodeen."

"You got an idea where he went?"

"No, except he had to travel south. He wouldn't have ridden back through town with the fire rousing everybody. No through roads to the west, and no way to get east across the creek without swimming between here and the ferry at the railroad bridge. Might be I can pick up his trail. Or find somebody who saw him."

"Slim chance, Linc."

"I know it. But it's a hell of a sight better than hanging fire in town, listening to Gladstone fulminate and watching Joe Perkins charge around like a bull in a china shop."

"I could come with you. Hell, we could organize a posse. . . ."

"No. Somebody with sense has got to tend to things here. And a posse would take too long, create too much fuss. Bodeen could be in San Francisco by the time we got one together."

Boze rubbed his bald spot, sniffing and blowing drip at the same time. "You want me to tell the mayor you're out hunting?"

"No point in not telling him."

"Anything else I should do?"

"Nose around, find out if anybody saw or heard anything." I took the presidential medal out of my pocket and showed it to him. "You ever see one of these before?"

He looked it over, shook his head. "Where'd you get it?"

"Right about where you're standing. I'd say whoever killed Pike dropped it during the struggle. It isn't the kind of thing Pike would have carried around."

"Don't seem like the kind of thing Bodeen would carry, either."

"No," I agreed. "No, it doesn't at that."

"You want me to show it around?"

"To everybody you talk to."

Doc had finished his preliminary examination of the body and was coming toward us. He said, "Killed the same way as Jeremy Bodeen, looks like. Beat up some first—bruises on his face, broken finger on one hand."

"Skin off his knuckles?" I asked.

"Some."

"So maybe he did some damage in return."

"Good chance of it, I'd say."

I showed Doc the medal; it was unfamiliar to him, too. Then I turned it over to Boze and went into the harness room, where I stripped out of my fire-ruined clothing and put on the shirt and trousers and cutaway coat Boze had brought. I checked the Bisley Colt, to make sure it was fully loaded, before I strapped it on.

My saddle and bridle were where they always were; I carried them out and asked Boze to outfit the chalk-eye. While he was doing that I made a quick search through Pike's clothing, on the chance that they contained something enlightening. But they didn't. Just a sack of Bull Durham, papers, matches, and three pennies.

I rode out through the rear doors, leaving Boze and Doc to their own unpleasant tasks. When I came around to the front, Verne Gladstone and Fred Horler and two other men were fifty yards away and closing fast on the livery. The mayor hailed me in his bullfrog voice; Horler yelled something.

Pretending not to hear, I kneed Rowdy and pounded away at a gallop.

CHAPTER 11

TULE Bend Road was deserted this time of morning, and so was the country road that connected San Rafael and Petaluma. Oak-furred ridges and rolling, dry-brown pastureland hemmed it on both sides, with the creek winding its tortuous way through the tule marshes over east. The sun was up now and already it had warmed the morning enough to melt some of the frost; steam rose off patches of grass, and thickly off the creek and its flanking mud flats.

Out here I had to ride at a fast trot, rather than a gallop, because last winter's heavy rains, constant wagon travel through the mud, and the baking heat of this past summer had combined to badly rut the road in places. Fatigue put a grittiness in my eyes, a dull ache in my temples. But there was more anger in me than anything else. If I had been feeding on gall and wormwood yesterday morning, this morning I was gorged with them.

It took me the better part of twenty minutes to reach the S.F. & N.P. swing bridge. There was a graveled wagon road that led in off the county road to the bridge, the bridgeman's shanty, and the old self-operated ferry. To the south, the right-of-way bulked up in a long gradual curve to the bridge; on the far side it made the same kind of curve northward, where it straightened out for the run past Tule Bend and on into Petaluma. The bridge itself was a bone of contention among some

local citizens. They said it jutted too far into the stream
and interfered with shipping, and there was talk of
replacing it with a drawbridge that could also be used
for pedestrian and wagon traffic. But nothing was likely
to be done about that for a good long while, if ever, the
railroad being what it was and the county politicians
being what they were.

The ferry landing was on the near side of the bridge,
between it and the bridgeman's shanty. It was not much
as ferries go—just a small barge large enough for a
wagon and horse or a handful of people, drawn back
and forth by means of a pair of underwater cables that
you had to work by hand. Ranchers and farmers over
east used it enough to warrant its upkeep. The boatmen
didn't like it, especially the steamer captains, because
they were concerned about those underwater cables.
There had never been any problem, though. The weight
of the cables kept them sunk into the bottom mud
except when they were being used. The steamers could
not go upstream except at high tide anyhow, on account
of the danger of their stern wheels foundering in the
mud.

When I neared the shanty I spied Pop Baker standing
on the creekbank at the rear. I rode on up to the
building and dismounted there and walked down to
where he was. The mist was heavy here; it had an eerie
look under the sun, like living things writhing in pain
and clinging desperately to the bridge, dying in the
day's gathering warmth. The tide was at flood and the
salt and tule-grass smells were sharp.

Pop had been bridgeman here from the day the first
train crossed after the bridge was finished in 1880. He
was tall and gangly, all arms and legs, with a nose like a
beak and white hair that had the look of feather-down

on a newborn chick; he reminded you of a big shore-
bird, the kind that poke around through the tules on
their long, spindly legs. He was bundled in coat and
gloves and cap, and he had a fishing pole in one hand
and a second stuck in the mud nearby, both lines
trailing out into the creek.

"Morning, Pop. Catch breakfast yet?"

"Not yet. What brings you out here so early?"

He hadn't seen the smoke or fireglow last night, nor
had anybody been by yet to bring him news of the fire;
elsewise he would have started clamoring right away for
a full report. Just as well, because I had no time to waste.

I said, "Looking for somebody who might have ridden
this way between three and four this morning. You hear
anyone use the ferry around that time?"

"Sure did. Not one man, though. Two."

That took me aback. "*Two* men on horseback?"

"You said it."

"Together?"

"Nope. Few minutes apart."

"Both crossing from this side?"

"Yep."

"You happen to see either of them?"

"First one woke me up but I didn't get out of bed,"
Pop said. "Did get up for a look when the second one
showed; hardly anybody ever uses the ferry that late
and I wondered what was goin' on. But it was too dark
to get a clear squint at him. Just a fellow on horseback."

"Thanks, Pop."

I went and got Rowdy and led him down to the ferry
landing. The barge was over on the far bank. I made
sure there was no creek traffic in sight before I hauled
the barge back across. Then I put the chalk-eye and

myself on board, closed the gate, and pulled us the seventy-five yards to the east shore.

The road that led away from the landing on this side was a narrow levee track through waist-high tangles of tules and cattails and salt grass. In the winter, when the rains were heavy, it was impassable. Even now it was so full of pocks and ruts that I had to let Rowdy pick his way along at not much more than a walk.

As I rode I thought over what Pop had told me. Two men, a few minutes apart. One following the other? That seemed the likeliest explanation. One of them figured to be Emmett Bodeen; but then who was the other? Was Bodeen the follower or the one being followed? And if one of them had killed Jacob Pike, as also seemed likely, which one was it?

I counted myself lucky that they had come this way, instead of continuing south on the main road. There were several towns and steamer landings in that direction—Bardells, Novato, Ignacio, Millers, San Rafael—and any number of escape routes by road, rail, or boat. Over east there were only a couple of hamlets, fewer roads and transportation points, a good deal of private and unsettled land, and the rugged Sonoma Mountains. By going that way, Bodeen or whoever was setting the course might be on his way to the Valley of the Moon or the Napa Valley or points east; or it could just be that he did not know his way around these parts very well and was traveling blind. In any case, I had at least a fair chance of tracking one or both men, and the knowledge took away some of my fatigue, gave me a fresh sense of purpose.

The levee road angled through the salt marshes for half a mile to Lakeville, where the creek began to straighten out for the last few miles of its route into San

Pablo Bay. From there I could go in one of three directions—on south to Sonoma Landing at the mouth of the creek, back north toward Petaluma, or east to Stage Gulch and the road into the Valley of the Moon. If my luck continued to hold, somebody in or around Lakeville would be able to give me an idea of which direction my quarry had taken. Otherwise, I would have to make an arbitrary choice.

It was coming on nine o'clock when I reached Lakeville. Once it had been part of General Vallejo's huge rancho, and had derived its name from a big pond, Laguna de Tolay, that had sat among the low hills nearby. In the years following the Bear Flag revolt, Vallejo had sold off all of this land; and in the sixties, a German immigrant named Bihler had drained the lagoon so he could plant acres of corn and potatoes. Nowadays there was not much to Lakeville other than the wharf Vallejo had built, a few houses, and Hobemeyer's General Store.

Hobemeyer was open for business—would have been since eight, if I knew old Leo. His was the only store within several miles, and he liked the feel of money more than most. I tied Rowdy to the hitchrail in front, next to a farm wagon drawn by a slab-sided bay mare, and went on inside.

Cluttered place, Hobemeyer's, with shadowy corners and over-stocked shelves and overflowing tables and counters. Tools, coils of rope, and other items hung from the ceiling beams. A dozen different savors vied with each other for dominance: smoked bacon, coffee, dried onions, pepper, beeswax, strong tobacco, cloth and drygoods, boot and saddle and harness leather. Against one wall a fat-bodied stove glowed cherry red and gave off pulsing waves of heat.

Old Leo Hobemeyer was nowhere in sight. Behind the main counter, Leo's chubby and pomaded son, Dolph, was waiting on a man I didn't know, a farmer in bib overalls and a straw hat. They both watched me as I approached the counter.

"Well—Constable Evans," Dolph said in his sly way. He greeted most men as if they were a cut below his level of intelligence, which was not so high as far as I could tell; and most women as if they were simpletons and he was doing them a favor by waiting on them. Nobody liked him much, including his father. Old Leo would have thrown him out long ago, I suspected, if he didn't suffer from the gout and need someone to run the store for him. "To what do we owe the honor?"

"Business matter, Dolph."

"More calamity in Tule Bend? You look as if you've been fighting a fire."

"Razor burn," I said shortly. He always did bring out the worst in me. "I'm looking for two men who rode through on the levee road sometime around four this morning."

Dolph and the farmer exchanged looks. "Do tell," Dolph said to me, and smiled like a bratty kid with a secret.

The farmer said, "Don't believe we've met, Mister. My name's Simon Fletcher. Bought a piece of land south of here last spring, moved my family up from the San Joaquin Valley."

I introduced myself and we shook hands.

"Say those men you're lookin' for was around here at four this morning?" Fletcher asked.

"That's right."

"Well, I was just tellin' Mr. Hobemeyer here, I heard shootin' around that time. Woke me and the wife up."

"What kind of shooting?"

"Pistol shots, sounded like. Half a dozen or more."

"One man firing or two trading shots? Could you tell?"

"Two different weapons, I'd say."

"Could you pinpoint the location?"

"South of my place, down toward Donahue Landing."

"Perhaps it was ghosts," Dolph said, and laughed. He had the damnedest laugh for a big man, squeaky and flatulent at the same time, like a mouse passing wind. "Donahue is filled with them, you know."

Fletcher didn't see the joke, such as it was. "No, sir," he said seriously, "that shootin' was real enough. Woke me and the missus up, like I say."

I asked, "You hear anything else after it stopped?"

He shook his head. "Last couple of shots sounded farther away, though."

"As if whoever was doing the firing was on horseback?"

"Yes, sir."

"Did you go out to investigate?"

"I wanted to, but my old woman wouldn't hear of it."

Dolph mouth-farted again. Neither Fletcher nor I paid him any attention.

"What about this morning?" I asked. "Before you came here?"

"Well, I took my wagon down that way, down to Donahue, but I didn't see anybody or anything."

Dolph snapped one of his galluses—another of his nettling habits—and asked me, "What did they do, Constable? The men you're after?"

I didn't answer him. Instead I nodded to Fletcher and turned for the door.

Behind me Dolph said, "If you're going to Donahue,

Constable, do watch out. The banshees are particularly fearsome this time of year."

Silly damned jackass. I went out and slammed the door behind me.

Mounted again, I rode on to the fork and took the road south toward Donahue Landing. Pistol shots in the marshes, pre-dawn . . . it had to be Bodeen and whoever the second rider was. Antagonists, that seemed certain now. No reason for the shooting, otherwise. But I still didn't know which was which, or why one had been following the other, or what the outcome of the gunplay had been, or where either or both men were now.

It was only about a mile to Donahue Landing. Or what was left of it, and that was not much after ten years of abandonment. The remains lay rotting alongside the creek—a ghost in that respect, though there had never been any superstitious talk that I was aware of about the place being haunted. That was just more of Dolph's sly mouth-farting.

The town had been built nearly twenty years ago by Peter Donahue, a business tycoon and the man responsible for installing the first street lights in San Francisco and for bringing decent short-line rail service to Sonoma County. He had built up the San Francisco & Northern Pacific, and planned originally to make Petaluma its northern terminus; but when city officials there refused him permission to run his railroad straight down Main Street, he had declared war on the town by laying track on the east side of the creek, south past Tule Bend to a new terminus below Lakeville—Donahue Landing, built from the ground up on cleared marshland and named after himself.

For a few years the company town had flourished. There had been a long wharf at the water's edge, a roundhouse beyond that allowed his trains to pull out alongside docking steamers and his crews to transfer freight from the boats, most of which he also owned, onto the cars for shipment to rail points throughout the county. He had put up houses, stores, a firehouse, docks, a saloon, a combination stable and Saturday-night dancehall, even a forty-room hotel called the Sonoma House and a one-room schoolhouse that served farm children and the sons and daughters of his employees. Passenger trains ran through there, too, filled with folks taking day excursions up from San Francisco.

Eventually, though, Peter Donahue healed his rift with the politicans in Petaluma, mainly because he kept on expanding his holdings by buying up other short-line roads, connecting them to the S.F. & N.P., and extending them into San Rafael and down to Point Tiburon. Passengers preferred the new, faster routes, and so did shippers; business at Donahue Landing fell off to almost nothing. So the old man, who had been about as sentimental as a wolf in a shearing pen, dismantled the town a building at a time and used barges to float the lumber and fixtures down to his new terminus at Tiburon. When he got done, there was nothing much left except the wharf, part of the dancehall, most of the roundhouse, a few abandoned homes, and a lot of bare foundations. That had been in 1882, ten years ago, and so far as I knew, nobody had ever tried to claim squatter's rights since. The only occupants of Donahue in all that time had been an occasional tramp and, likely, whole platoons of rats.

The road wiggled its way along between marshland on the west and a mix of pastureland and low, wooded hills on the east. I met no one, saw nothing as I neared the ruins that testified to a recent gunfight. Ahead, finally, I could see what was left of the crumbling right-of-way where the S.F. & N.P. spur had cut away in a long northward diagonal from the town. There was a screen of trees along the near side of the landing's wagon road, and when I came around them, onto the overgrown track, the old tycoon's leavings were visible.

Storms and salt-erosion had knocked down all but one of the abandoned houses and two walls of the dancehall; the only building still standing whole was the heavy black-wood roundhouse, and it would not be for long: part of its roof sagged near collapse. Pigweed and salt grass and swamp oak grew over the site, reclaiming it for the marsh. Boggy backwaters clogged with tules and cattails had begun to encroach on the land as well.

The long wharf and the remnants of the steamer docks were bent and broken jumbles of boards sinking into the ragged stands of tules along the shoreline. Southward over the creek a pelican flew screeching above a melon boat that was making its ponderous way downstream toward San Pablo Bay. Otherwise the sun-struck morning was still, windless, with no movement within the range of my vision.

After fifty yards, marsh growth completely obliterated the track, so that I had to pick a random course toward the center of town. There were no signs of other recent passage through here, but a feeling of unease began to work inside me just the same. I loosened the Bisley in its holster, let my hand rest on the handle.

Marsh sounds, faint but audible now—insects, a frog croaking, small-animal rustlings. From some hidden place near the creek, a wild mallard rose quacking. I stood up in the stirrups, trying to see farther ahead over the tall swamp growth. The roundhouse was a hundred yards away, at an angle to my right. I reined the chalk-eye over that way, around a mound of grass-covered rubble where a building had once stood.

In that instant, something slashed the air a few inches from my right cheek. It caused me to jerk my head, then froze me for an instant—just long enough for a hollow echo to roll over the ruins like the crack of doom, and for me to realize that what had gone by was a bullet.

Somebody was shooting at me with a rifle!

CHAPTER 12

ROWDY balked, dancing sideways—and a second bullet whipped past me at a lower angle and struck him somewhere on the hindquarters. He screamed, reared straight up on his back legs and then went over and down hard on his right side. The weight of him would have crushed my leg, and perhaps the rest of me when he flopped onto his back, except that I had long since thrown myself out of the saddle. Grass and pigweed and wet spongy earth cushioned my fall, so that I was able to roll clear of him fast when he went down. Noise seemed to swell in my ears like air pumping into a balloon—Rowdy's scream and the hammering echo of the second shot and the grunt and gasp of my breathing.

I fetched up belly-flat in a matted tangle of tules and fumbled for the Bisley at my hip. It had not been jarred loose in the fall and roll; I yanked it free, thumbed the hammer back. Through a haze of sweat I saw that the chalk-eye was not badly hurt. He had got his legs under him, and when he was up, a few seconds later, he loped off the way we had come.

There hadn't been any more firing, just those two rounds while I was up on Rowdy's back. The shots had come from somewhere in front and to one side of me . . . inside or near the roundhouse, I thought. Cautiously I raised up for a look in that direction, but from down on the ground like this I could see only the

106

upper half of the building. There was nothing else to see, except for a cloud of blackbirds that had been scared up by the shots and were winging away over the creek.

I lay still for a time, dry-mouthed, listening. Once the blackbirds were gone, there was utter silence. Even the insects were quiet now.

The place where I lay was one of the swampy back-waters. The upper half of my body was on a pad of tules, the lower half in black mud that made little sucking sounds whenever I moved. Swamp flies and mosquitoes had begun to swarm around me, to bite at my face and neck. The bog smell in my nostrils was thick, fetid, like an outhouse on a hot day.

At an angle to where I was, near where the remains of the long wharf were sinking into the creek, a weeping willow stood with its low-hanging branches brushing the ground. I dragged myself through the tules, out onto firmer, drier earth, and began to crawl toward the willow, stopping every few feet to listen again. Once I thought I heard the faraway nicker of a horse that was not Rowdy, but the sound wasn't repeated.

It took me the better part of ten minutes to get into the dappled shade under the willow. I stood up slow behind the bole, parted the branches just enough so I could peer out. From this vantage point I had a better look at the front and west sides of the roundhouse. One of the big engine doors was gone, the other standing closed; as far as I could tell, nothing moved in the murkiness inside. Nor was there movement outside anywhere. The creek was empty now, the melon boat and the pelican both gone.

Between where I was and the roundhouse doors, the ground supported marshy growth and not much else. I judged the distance at about seventy-five yards. Hell of a long run in the face of a rifle: a man did not have to be a marksman to hit a running target on open ground like that. I worked some spit through the dryness in my mouth, trying to make up my mind. I could not stay here all day. And I was damned if I would go crawling back through the bog, hunt for the chalk-eye, and then ride off for help. Even if help were close by and easy to find, which it wasn't, it would be the same as running scared; and if there was one thing I was not, it was a coward. Besides, there was the fire of rage in me, the hot taste of it on the back of my tongue.

I was still thinking about risking a zig-zag run to the roundhouse when the horse and rider came plunging out of the shadows inside.

The suddenness of it held me motionless for a couple of seconds, gawking. By the time I slapped through the clinging screen of branches, into the open where I could see more clearly, he was better than a hundred yards away on a course toward the road.

Sorrel horse, and the man stretched out over the saddle with head tucked down and left arm flopping loose at his side, as if it might be broken or injured in some way: splotches of red-brown staining the shoulder and sleeve of his light-colored coat that might be blood. The horse looked like any sorrel, nothing distinctive about it from a distance; and I could not see the rider's face, or enough of him the way he was wrapped low around the animal's neck to even tell his size. Dark hair, denim trousers, tan coat with those red-brown splotches . . . those were the only things I could make out for sure.

Hot temper and frustration sent me to one knee, led me to squeeze off two rounds from the Bisley even though he was well out of handgun range. The reports rolled over the marsh, faded, and when the afterechoes were gone all I could hear was the far-off muffled pound of the sorrel's hooves.

The thought came to me then, belatedly, that I made a fine target kneeling out here in the open for anybody still forted up inside the roundhouse. I flattened out in the grass. Lay there for a time, feeling helpless and foolish, listening to the hoofbeats diminish to silence.

Nobody else in the roundhouse, I thought. He would have fired on me long since if there was. Just the same, I raised up slow, watching that dark opening where the horse and rider had emerged.

Nothing happened. Seemed certain now that nothing else was going to.

On my feet again, I scanned the terrain to the north. No sign of the man on the sorrel. No sign of Rowdy, either. The chalk-eye would not have wandered far—he wasn't the kind of horse to bolt and run for home. But by the time I found him, it would be too late to have a hope of catching up to my would-be assassin. And what if Rowdy was hurt worse than I had thought? Hell! If I could pick up the man's trail at all, it would be cool or already cold.

I kept looking at the roundhouse. One man, hurt, on a sorrel horse. Bodeen? But then where was his brother's roan? And where was the other man?

I had a little debate with myself—find the chalk-eye first or investigate the roundhouse—and the round-house won. With the Bisley on cock, I walked over there at an angle to the rectangular opening where the one engine door had been. When I got to the half that was still standing I eased along its warped boards, put my head around the edge and peered inside.

Sections of the roof had collapsed and there was enough sunlight coming in through the gaps to dilute the gloom, crowd the shadows back into corners of the cavernous interior. Grass and weeds had grown up through the cinder-strewn flooring, in places obscuring the debris that littered it in pieces and mounds. Empty workbenches made bulky, skeletal shapes along the walls. The black engine pits yawned like doorways into Satan's lair.

Soft-footed, I slid around the door and inside. Stood still for a minute—the rank-smelling space looked and felt empty—and then began to make my way forward. The turntable had been removed, I saw, although some of the machinery that had operated it was still there, pocked and corroded from the salt moisture. The engine pits were choked with the same sort of debris that cluttered the floor: chunks of roofing lathe and tarpaper, shattered timbers and loose boards, lengths of steel, rusting tackle, twisted things I couldn't name.

At the rear were two windows, the glass long ago broken out, framing bright daylight beyond. I moved toward them, being careful of where I put my boots. I was closing on the nearest window when something red and green caught my eye atop one of the workbenches. I changed direction to see what it was.

Horse blanket, made of wool and dyed the two colors—fairly new, fairly clean. When I took a closer look I saw the blood. Big dried splotch in one place, streaks and spots elsewhere on the fabric. He had been wounded, all right. Shot in that little skirmish last night and too badly hurt or too weak to ride any farther, he had come in here with the sorrel and spread his blanket before he passed out—that seemed the most likely explanation. Then, a while ago, he had heard or seen me coming, recognized me or just plain panicked, and pumped those two shots in my direction. Had to be because he was hurt, in need of doctoring, that he had ridden out instead of holding fast to make sure his bullets had done their work.

But that still did not give me a clue to his identity, or to what had happened to the second man. Mortally wounded in the gunfight, lying dead along the road or here in Donahue? Or just wounded and holed up somewhere else close by? Or had he got away clean and unhurt?

Scurrying sound behind me. I spun around, crouching . . . just in time to see a big gray shape burrow under a pile of rubble. Marsh rat. Some of them, this one included, grew as big as cats. They repelled me at the best of times; here, as tensed up as I was, I felt my gorge rise. I had spent enough time in here, breathed enough of the foul, rot-smelling air.

The blanket was evidence, so I folded it carefully, with the bloodstains on the inside, and put it under my arm. Then I made a quick check of the area to see if the man had left any other traces of himself. He hadn't. Finally I went ahead to the near window, leaned my head out for a look at what lay to the rear of the roundhouse.

What I saw back there was death.

The hairs went up on the nape of my neck; a sudden gnawing began under my breastbone that was nothing at all like a hunger pang. I gripped the rotted sill with my free hand, staring.

Storage shed, half crumbled now, and to one side of it a swamp oak that had been struck by lightning once, a long time ago, for its bole was split and fire-scarred. And from one of its branches, a man hanging by the neck—*another* dead man, strung up the same way as Jeremy Bodeen and Jacob Pike.

Victim number three.

The corpse was facing away from me: I could not tell from here who he was. But I had a sudden feeling, a bad feeling—what Ivy would call a foreboding—as to this one's identity. I pouched the Bisley and clambered out through the window opening, walked slow past the shed and around the oak to where I could look straight up into the hanged man's black-mottled face. And the bad feeling stayed with me, like a slow poison, because the face was just the one I had been afraid I would see.

This dead man was Emmett Bodeen.

CHAPTER 13

BITTERLY, I cut him down—the third time in five days I'd had to do that kind of disagreeable job.

There was caked blood on the side of his head, more caked blood above his right shoulder blade: two bullet wounds, neither of which looked to have been fatal. But if he'd been riding when he was shot, the loads would have knocked him out of his saddle and probably rendered him unconscious. Even a wounded man could do pretty much as he pleased with an unconscious foe.

The backside of Bodeen's clothing was torn and grass-stained, and there were rope fibers on the front of his coat, bruises and lacerations on his hands and forearms. Dragged here face up from wherever he was shot, I thought, and then strung up. No wonder that crazy son of a bitch had been too weak to ride any farther last night.

But why go through all that? Why not just put another bullet into Bodeen where he lay? Why the driving urge to hang him, as he had hanged the other two?

I examined Bodeen's knuckles. The contusions on them were from the dragging; they were not the kind of skin-scrapes that come from a fist fight. No fight marks on his face, either. Jacob Pike *had* been fight-marked, though, and had likely marked his attacker some too. If I needed any more proof that Emmett Bodeen was innocent of Pike's murder, there it was.

The same killer in all three cases, then: the man on

113

the sorrel horse. A good bet he was also the prowler I had tangled with—that he had been after Pike on Saturday night too. Twice now I had come close to being another of his victims: I had no doubt that he would have hanged me on Saturday if Pike and Badger in tandem hadn't scared him off. And he would have done the same to me today, if one of those rifle slugs had punctured my hide and put me out of commission long enough.

Bodeen's pockets were what I examined next. And what I found in one of them cleared up the robbery part of last night's muddle: money, more than six hundred dollars in greenbacks. It was Bodeen who had broken into the Far West offices and Fred Horler's cashbox. He had set the fire inside the saddlery, too; not only did his description fit the man Walt Barber had seen running away, his right hand smelled of kerosene. Kerosene gets into the pores if you don't take time to wash it off right after it spills on you, and the smell lingers for a long time.

Straightening, I put the six hundred dollars into my own pocket. I was thinking that now I had enough information to pretty much piece together last night's sequence of events. Must have gone this way:

Some time past midnight, Bodeen broke into the Far West office and stole the money. But he had also worked up a hate for me and Boze and the town-at-large, because of the way he'd been treated and the way his brother had died. So he went from the milling company to Sam McCullough's place—the nearest one to where Jeremy Bodeen had died—and started the fire.

His intention then was to take his brother's roan from the livery and ride out. But he got to the stable at about the same time as the madman was making *his* escape, on foot or already on horseback, after hanging Jacob Pike. Bodeen went inside the barn, spied Pike's corpse, figured out that the man he'd just seen must have killed his brother too, quick-saddled the roan, and gave chase.

He was a few minutes behind the madman at the ferry; finally caught up with him somewhere over this way. A challenge, maybe—an exchange of shots. Both men hit, but Bodeen's wounds were the more critical: mortal, in fact. For his own reasons, the madman put a rope around Bodeen and dragged him in here to lynch him. The shooting scrape must have taken place close by; no point in dragging Bodeen far, or to go far to find shelter for himself and his horse.

Why?

Who?

Well, his killing streak was finished now, by God, one way or another. His wound had to be serious; he had lost a lot of blood, judging from the stains on that blanket. Chances were he could not ride far. And even if he managed to get home he couldn't hide a gunshot wound and a marked face from friends, relatives, neighbors—not for long.

I left Bodeen's corpse lying there and went hunting for the chalk-eye. Took me fifteen minutes to find him. He had drifted in among the trees at the joining of the Donahue wagon road and the main road, and he was standing there, calm as you please, nuzzling grass. The rifle bullet had raked a shallow furrow across his croup, about an inch and a half long; it hadn't even bled much. He let me walk right up to him but he fought me when I got up on his back, frog-stepping and rearing, as if it were my fault he had been stung and frightened. I had to work at him and talk to him to get him gentled, and at that he went dauncy on me twice more before I coaxed him back behind the roundhouse.

But he would not go near Bodeen's body; and if I had tried to rope it on his back he would have gone wild and I'd have had a real fight on my hands. There was nothing to do but leave the corpse and send somebody back for it.

I found the irregular swath through the marsh growth where the madman had dragged Bodeen, and followed it, and as I expected it led out to the road. I got down there to have a look around. Some spots of dried blood but no shell casings or anything else that might have been helpful. There was no sign of Jeremy Bodeen's swaybacked roan. That old mossyback could have wandered five miles by now, all the way down to Sonoma Landing or all the way up to Petaluma.

I rode to the nearest ranch—owned by a cattleman I knew slightly named Alvin Smith—and told him as much as I had to and then asked him if he and one of his helpers would take a wagon to Donahue, load on Bodeen's corpse, and deliver it to Hobemeyer's General Store. Alvin was not keen on the idea but I got him to agree to it, and also to agree not to say anything to anyone once it was done.

When I returned to Lakeville I found old Leo Hobemeyer behind the counter in his store. Which was a relief. He was much easier to deal with than his sly fop of a son, especially after I promised him five dollars for keeping Emmett Bodeen's remains out of sight until further notice.

My stomach had started to give me hell: It was well past noon and I had not eaten anything since supper last night. Not that I had any appetite, after my experiences in Donahue; it was just that the cavity needed filling, for fuel to keep me going. I bought some jerky and a couple of apples and a bunch of grapes, and a bottle of Edward's Cream Ale to wash it all down with.

Then I went hunting.

I didn't bag a damned thing. I did not even get a sniff of the deadly game I was after.

I talked to people in and around Lakeville. I rode as far east as Stage Gulch and the Valley of the Moon road, as far north as General Vallejo's Adobe rancho outside Petaluma; questioned every traveler I saw, talked to men working in the fields, stopped at farmhouses and cattle pens. Nobody had seen the wounded man on the sorrel horse. It was as though he'd vanished into thin air after leaving Donahue.

But the truth of it was, he either lived close by or he had holed up somewhere to wait for nightfall. The second possibility struck me as the most likely. There were hundreds of places to hide in the Lakeville-Donahue area, both on public and private land—groves of trees, hollows, brush-choked defiles, even a cave or two. Anyone who knew the area could find a safe place with little difficulty.

Some before dusk, I was back in Lakeville. Dog-tired but too stubborn to give up just yet. I waited there, out back of Hobemeyer's store, until half an hour past dark, on the slim hope that the madman might have enough brass to show himself on one of the county roads after leaving his hiding place. But he was too cunning for that. The only two people who passed through while I was there were local residents with lawful reasons for being out after nightfall.

I called it quits finally; the chalk-eye was cranky and I was too weary to do any more senseless prowling. I took the levee road, and when I had ferried us across I roused Pop Baker out of an after-supper doze—one last little prayer on my part that went unanswered. Pop had not seen the wounded man on the sorrel horse, either.

It was coming on nine o'clock when Rowdy and I trudged into Tule Bend. Tule Bend Road was deserted and so was south Main. The livery barn stood dark, closed up tight—nobody around. Morton Brandeis must have shut down temporarily, on account of Jacob Pike's murder. Which surprised me; Morton was neither a fearful nor a compassionate man. It nettled me some, too, because now I would have to take Rowdy up to the Union Hotel and beg a stall and feed for him at their stables.

The burned-out leavings of this morning's fire bulked up along the creekbank, all broken and jagged-edged, like ravaged black skeletons in a moonlit graveyard. The town might have *been* a graveyard, too, for all the life it appeared to contain. Main Street was a deserted lamplit path through it, not a soul in sight; except for lights in houses and saloons, the place might have been abandoned—a plague town whose citizens had all fled for their lives. Well, in a way it *was* a plague town now. Only the plague was murder, not a pestilential disease, and the citizens had retreated inside, behind locked and barred doors and with weapons close to hand.

There were two men I needed to talk to before I gave in to my body's demand for rest—Obe Spencer and Doc Petersen. Boze could wait until morning, unless he had found out something important in my absence; if he had, either Obe or Doc would know about it.

Spencer's Undertaking Parlor was closest, so I stopped there first. Obe lived on the premises, upstairs—alone

since his wife passed away two years ago and the last of
his sons moved out. There was lamplight in the upstairs
front window, behind a drawn shade. I got down at the
gate and went up onto the porch and gave the handle
of his doorbell a twist. He didn't answer right away—not
that I blamed him—and I had to work the bell twice
more before he finally came down.

Without unlatching the door he demanded in wary
tones, "Who's there?"

"Linc Evans. Let me in, Obe."

He let me in. There was a big Colt Frontier in his
right hand, which he allowed to hang down at his side
when he saw me; but he did not let go of it while we
talked. And Obe and I had known each other all my life
and most of his.

"You find him, Linc?" he asked first thing. "You find
that Emmett Bodeen?"

"I found him, all right. Over in Donahue. He's dead."

"Dead? Mean you killed him?"

"No. Somebody hung him, same as with his brother
and Jacob Pike."

"Good Lord!" Obe's face was white now, the fear in
his eyes bright and moist. "Mean Bodeen didn't kill
Pike?"

"No. The same person did all three murders."

"Who, Linc? You know who?"

"Not yet. But I do know he's hurt, wounded in a
gunfight with Bodeen." I gave him a brief account of
the day's events and my surmises.

"Somebody who lives *here?*" he said. "Somebody we
all know?"

"That's how it looks."

"Jesus, Mary and Joseph."

"Anything happen today I should know about?"

"Let me think." His free hand shook a little as he passed it over his face. "Verne Gladstone sent for Sheriff Perkins again, but he still hadn't come as of sundown. Probably won't be here until tomorrow, now."

"That all?"

"Well . . . just loose talk."

"What kind of loose talk?"

He said, "About you, the way you been handling things," and he would not look at me as he spoke.

"So it's out in the open now. Folks blaming me."

"Only some put the blame on you. Others . . . well, you're only one man. And Boze is just a part-time deputy."

"I've done all anyone can do," I said with some bitterness. "So has Boze. What does the town want? Martial law?"

"Armed patrols. Sheriffs' or citizens'."

"Oh, fine. Fine! Vigilante days again."

"Lordy, Linc, *something's* got to be done."

"I told you, the man responsible is wounded. How far can a wounded man go, how long can he hide? It's only a matter of time until he's identified and caught."

"Some won't want to wait, once word about Emmett Bodeen gets out."

"Word's not going to get out, not for a while," I said. "I swore Alvin Smith and the Hobemeyers to secrecy and I'm doing the same with you. First thing in the morning, no later than first light, I want you to take your hearse over to Lakeville and pick up the body and bring it back here."

"Alone? You want me to go all that way *alone?*"

"Obe, nobody's going to jump you on public roads!"

"That's what you say. I'm not going alone. You can't force me against my will."

I wanted to take hold of him and shake him; I had precious little patience left, as tired as I was. But how could you blame a man for fearing for his life at a time like this? You couldn't, really. It was every man's right to protect himself.

I said, "Ask one of your sons to go with you. Will you do it that way, with company?"

He thought about it, nodded reluctantly. "But what if somebody sees us, asks who we got in the hearse?"

"Say it's a farmer who died of natural causes. Man new to the area. No one will see the body if you keep it covered. Just make sure you keep quiet about who it really is—and that your son does too."

"What about Mayor Gladstone and the sheriff? You going to tell them?"

"I don't know yet."

"Word will get out anyway, sooner or later," Obe said. "Too many people know already."

"Just make sure you're not the one who lets it out."

"I will. I mean, I won't."

"All right. By the time word does get around, we'll have the guilty party locked up in jail."

"If you say so," he said, but I could tell that he didn't believe it. For that matter I was not sure I believed it myself.

Doc Petersen's house was in the next block, and he was also home—and not half so wary or frightened as Obe and the rest of the town seemed to be. Doc had served in the Union Army during the Civil War as a medic on more than one battlefield, Bull Run being one of them. After what he had been through in those years, he had told me once, there was not much fear of death left inside him.

I took him into my confidence, as I had Obe. By

necessity. But of all those who knew about Emmett Bodeen's murder, I trusted Doc the most to keep silent.

He said when I was done talking, "So you want me to watch for anybody comes looking for treatment for a gunshot wound. Well, nobody has so far today, I can tell you that."

"I don't think he'll come himself," I said. "He's too smart for that. What he might do is send somebody in his place, on the pretense of sickness or some kind of accident. You'll have to be on the lookout for that too."

"Don't worry, my boy. I'm too old to be gulled easily. You'll know right away if my suspicions are aroused."

"Thanks, Doc."

"Don't let Gladstone and that lard-bottom Perkins push you around to their way of thinking tomorrow," he said. "Things will only get worse if you do."

I did not give him any false assurances, as I had Obe; there was no need with a man of Doc's caliber. I just nodded and left him to the rest of his evening.

No sense in my going home to sleep. Ivy slept soft, and if I tried to sneak into the house she would hear me and bombard me with foolish questions and opinions. I rode instead to the Union Hotel stables, turned Rowdy over to the hostler there, with instructions to tend to the bullet nick on his croup, and then trudged back to the Odd Fellows Hall and let myself into the office and collapsed on a cot in one of the holding cells. I just did manage to get my boots off before I fell asleep.

CHAPTER 14

THE weather changed during the night—of a sudden, the way it often does around here. Fog and low clouds blew in from the ocean thirty miles away, herded by an icy November wind. The cold woke me around five; I got up and fetched blankets from the other two cells and heaped them over me, but I could not get back to sleep. I lay there thinking on things, without much consequence, until first light. Then I got up for good, built a fire in the stove and brewed some coffee. I was drinking my third cup and scraping dried swamp mud off my trousers when Boze came in just past seven.

He seemed relieved to see me, though the relief didn't last beyond my account of what had transpired in and around Donahue Landing. He rubbed his bald spot, looking unhappy, and said about the same as Obe and Doc had last night: "We can't keep the lid on long, Linc. Mayor Gladstone's got a nose like a bloodhound; he'll sniff it out about Emmett Bodeen before the day's through."

"Maybe not," I said. "Depends on how soon Joe Perkins gets here and how much hurdy-gurdy he creates when he does."

"Perkins will want to bring in deputies for a house-to-house search. What do you bet?"

"No bet."

"If he does it, there'll be hell to pay."

"I know it. But the only way to keep him from doing it is to arrest the murderer ourselves."

"Maybe the son of a bitch is already dead," Boze said. "Died of his wounds on the way home or after he got there."

"Sure, that's possible."

"But not likely. Be too easy that way."

"At the least he's holed up," I said. "And if he's holed up, he's not going to be hanging anybody else. Look at it that way."

"Yeah. You got any ideas where to go lookin'?"

"No. I was hoping maybe you found out something yesterday that'll give us one."

He shook his head. "I must of showed that presidential medal to fifty people. Couple had seen one before but not around Tule Bend."

"Nobody saw or heard what went on at the livery?"

"Not that owned up to it." Then he frowned and said, "I don't know that it means anything, but there is one funny thing that happened."

"What's that?"

"Well, it's Morton Brandeis. I sent word up to Morton's house after you left yesterday morning, about Pike being hanged in the livery. Morton said he'd be down but he never showed up. Later on, after nine, Joel Pennywell saw him ridin' east out of town with a carpetbag tied to his saddle."

That *was* odd. "You talk to Lucy Brandeis or Maude Seeley about it?"

"Maude. She said Lucy is too sick to have visitors. Said Morton had business in the Napa Valley. But she was tight-lipped and sour about it, like she'd been sucking lemons. Practically shut the door in my face when I asked what his business in Napa was."

"He come back to town later on?"

"Not as far as I know."

"Who closed up the livery?"

"I did. I didn't know what else to do."

"What about the horses?"

"Owners came and got some. I took the rental nags up to the Union Hotel stables."

I nodded, pacing a little now.

"What gets me," Boze said, "is why Morton would leave town without stoppin' at the livery. Pike worked for him—that's one thing. And you'd think he would want to see what damage was done, make some arrangements to keep the place open or else shut it down himself."

"You'd think."

Boze was silent for a time. Then he said, "You don't think Morton had anything to do with the hangings, do you? Hell, we've known him most of our lives . . . ."

"You can know somebody a long time and not know him at all . . . what goes on inside his head. But no, I don't see how he could be mixed up in it. He isn't the wounded man who fired on me in Donahue, not if he was here in Tule Bend yesterday morning."

"Well, maybe he's over in the Napa Valley, just like Maude said."

"Maybe." But it still bothered me, and I thought that I would have a talk with Maude Seeley myself later on. "Anything else happen yesterday that I should know about?"

"Well . . . there was a lot of talk."

"Citizen patrols? Obe mentioned that last night."

"About you and me, too. Especially you."

"Uh-huh. Making you and me the scapegoats."

"More than that."

"Such as what?"

Boze looked uncomfortable. "You and me never talked about it," he said, "and I don't like to talk about it now. It's none of my business nor anybody else's. But that don't stop some from waggin' their tongues."

I knew what was coming, now. "Hannah Dalton," I said.

"That's it. Bluenoses don't like it that you're keepin' company with her. They say she's got you so fuddled you don't know which end is up."

"Well, confound them!"

"You want to know who's doin' the talking?"

"No. Better I don't. Bullshit is what it is, Boze."

"Sure, I know that. But some believe it and there's nothing anybody can say to change their minds."

"I suppose they want me to resign."

"Or the town council to replace you."

"Who with? You?"

"Hell no. Murray Conrad."

"Dandy choice." Murray Conrad was a former county deputy who had worked under Joe Perkins during his first term and then quit when his uncle died and left him the family chicken ranch up near Petaluma. He was a decent sort, Murray, but none too bright and a little heavy-handed in his methods. As a peace officer, he was in the same barnyard as Perkins. "What does the mayor say about all the talk?"

"You know how he is. Told me he was—quote—reservin' judgment for the time being—unquote."

I was starting to get riled again. "To hell with him. To hell with the rest of them too. Maybe I *ought* to resign . . . maybe move out of Tule Bend for good."

"Easy, Linc. It's not everybody that's talkin' behind your back. Just a few."

"That's how it starts, with just a few."

Boze fell silent, I suppose because he was afraid of getting me even hotter than I was. I sat at my rolltop and scowled out at the fog roving past the window, until I cooled down again. More and more lately, I seemed prone to flying off the handle. I had cause, God knew, but that didn't justify it. It was as if there was more eating at my vitals than just the murders and how folks were reacting to them and to me—something I could not put the right name to yet, just as I couldn't put a name to the madman who had killed the Bodeen brothers and Jacob Pike.

Over by the stove, Boze stood watching me. I could feel the stare of his eyes. I looked up and said, "Hell, Boze, I apologize. No reason to take it out on you."

"Nothing to apologize for," he said. "Were I you, I'd feel the same way."

"Suppose we go get some breakfast? I haven't eaten since—"

I did not finish the sentence—and we did not go get some breakfast—because the door banged open just then and a too-familiar bullfrog voice said, "Well, Lincoln, I heard you were back. Why didn't you report to me last night, eh?"

Mayor Verne Gladstone. And right behind him was Sheriff Joe Perkins, decked out in a loud checked suit and almost as corpulent as the mayor from all the pig's knuckles and fatty beefsteak he tucked away.

The rest of the morning was a loss. I had to tell my Donahue story twice to satisfy the mayor and Perkins and then submit to a long volley of questions, most of them inane. I manufactured half-truths to cover up my finding of Emmett Bodeen's hanged corpse, and al-

lowed as how Bodeen must have lit a shuck for parts
unknown after getting into the shootout with his brother's killer. As for the stolen money, which I had put into
the office safe last night, I said that I had found it near
the roundhouse in Donahue, just lying in a patch of
grass where Bodeen must have lost it. Everything else I
told pretty much as it had happened and according to
my speculations.

Perkins was all for bringing in a wagonload of deputies and mounting a house-to-house search, just as Boze
had prophesied. The mayor was against that, but only
because he couldn't bring himself to believe that one of
his friends or neighbors was a homicidal madman. The
two of them argued about it as if Boze and I weren't
even there. Then two other members of the town council showed up, one of them being Fred Horler, and I
had to tell my story a third time, and get the six
hundred dollars out of the safe for Fred to count twice
before he was satisfied that it was all there, *and* listen to
another heated argument that all but excluded me. My
temper was so short by then I had to take my pipe out
and bite down hard on the stem to keep angry words
from spilling out.

What they all finally decided was that Perkins would
ask "discreet" questions around town and see what he
could find out, and that the rest of us would do the
same. If none of us turned up anything definite by four
o'clock, we would all meet back here and compare notes
and make a final decision as to what would be done
next.

It was a reasonable enough plan, except that Perkins
did not know the meaning of the word discreet and was
bound to stir things up even more than they already
were. If he found out anything important, it would be

by sheer accident. And his presence, if not his tactics, would make it more difficult for Boze and me to accomplish much of anything worthwhile.

It was after eleven before we were able to get away. I needed to put some food in me first thing. Boze had eaten earlier and wasn't hungry, he said, so I asked him to go to Obe Spencer's and find out if Obe had done as I'd told him and brought back Emmett Bodeen's body. Then I went to the Germany Cafe and filled the hole in my belly with eggs and sausage and two helpings of potato pancakes.

Boze arrived just as I was finishing my coffee. Obe had brought the body back, all right, and without incident.

From the cafe, we went our separate ways. Morton Brandeis's sudden disappearance was still nettling my mind, and because I had nowhere better to go yet, I walked up to Morton's house on First Street and rang the front bell. Nobody answered. Which was peculiar, because Lucy Brandeis was bed-ridden and had not left the house since she'd taken ill; and her sister seldom left her alone for a minute.

I rang the bell twice more, then went around to the rear and knocked on the door there and called out a couple of times, also without getting a response. When I came back to the front again I thought I saw the parlor curtain move, as if somebody had been looking out from behind it. If Maude and Lucy *were* home, there was only one reason I could see for Maude not answering the door: neither she nor Lucy wanted to talk about Morton, especially not to me.

On a hunch, I walked back to Main and entered the North Coast Bank and spoke to Waldo Thomas, the president. He didn't want to reveal confidential information about one of his customers, but I worked on him for ten minutes until he gave in and told me what I wanted to know.

Before leaving town yesterday morning, Morton had drawn out exactly half of what was in his account—more than three thousand dollars. And he had taken the money in cash, greenbacks.

Waldo didn't know why; Morton had not volunteered any explanation and Waldo hadn't asked. He had no idea where Morton might have gone, either.

What the hell?

Outside, I crossed the street on a point back toward First and the Brandeis house. I would get to the bottom of this with Maude Seeley, even if it meant using some of Joe Perkins' bullying tactics. I still couldn't see how Morton's actions and disappearance could have anything to do with the hangings; but until I found out just what they did have to do with, I wasn't ruling out any possibility.

But I didn't make a second visit to the Brandeis house straightaway. I got sidetracked by Ervin Ramsey.

Ramsey was a little chicken turd of a man with a mean spirit and a disposition to match. He worked as a glazier, among other things, and he was driving his big A-bedded glass wagon down Main as I came upstreet toward First. We noticed each other at about the same time. One of his disagreeable, lopsided grins appeared and he called out, "Hold on there, Constable," and then reined his horse over my way and to a stop.

I scowled at him. Neither of us had much use for the other. I had thrown him in jail overnight once for public intoxication and he had taken that and his twenty-dollar fine more bitterly than most.

"What is it, Ramsey?"

"Know where I'm headed?"

"How would I? And I don't give a hoot, either."

"Sure you do. Up to your lady friend's."

"What?"

"Miss Hannah Dalton. Or is it Mrs.? I just can't keep it straight about that woman and all the men in her life."

"What the hell are you talking about?"

"Don't you know, Constable? I figured she'd of come runnin' to tell you about it first thing, the two of you being so chummy and all."

"Spit it out or swallow it."

"Why, then, I guess you *don't* know," Ramsey said, and his grin widened out like a wolf's over a bloody sheep carcass. "Somebody chucked a big rock through her front window last night. Smashed it to smithereens. That's why she sent for me."

A tightness came into my chest, so that I began to have a little trouble breathing. My hands curled into fists.

"But that ain't all," Ramsey said. "Way I heard it, there was a message tied to that rock. 'Course I don't know what was on it, but I can imagine. Yes sir, I sure can imagine what that message must of said."

CHAPTER 15

HANNAH's parlor window had been smashed, all right:
only a few jagged shards of glass still remained in the
frame. She had found a piece of plywood somewhere
and fixed it up on the inside, to keep out the cold wind
that blew across the bluff. Seeing the shards and the
plywood pushed my dander up even higher. If I found
out who was responsible . . .

Ramsey swore he hadn't done it, swore he didn't know
who had. Maybe that was the truth and maybe it wasn't;
the only way to tell for sure was to beat up on him some,
and I was not ready for that—not yet. So I had ordered
him to delay an hour before he brought the new pane
of glass Hannah had ordered—I wanted to talk to her
alone, without him and his flappy ears around—and
then I had come straight here myself.

I climbed onto the front porch, twisted the bell. The
door had leaded-glass panes in it and I saw her draw
the curtain aside briefly to see who it was. At least she
was being cautious. A few seconds passed before she
opened the door. She wore a silk shirtwaist and a figured
cloth skirt, clothing that showed off her comely figure
to good advantage, and she had braided her hair rather
than piled it atop her head—a style that made her look
younger than her thirty years. But this was a business
matter, not a social call; I felt none of the yearning that
filled me on those nights with her on the rear porch.

She said in grave tones, "Good morning, Lincoln."

132

"Hannah."

"You look tired. You haven't been hurt again?"

"No. I expect you know why I'm here."

"The window. I had hoped you wouldn't find out."

"Why, for heaven's sake? Why didn't you come and tell me about it?"

"You have enough on your mind. And I knew you would be angry. You're angry now."

"Well, why shouldn't I be? Aren't you?"

"No. It isn't important."

"The hell it isn't . . . excuse me, but it *is* important. Malicious mischief is a crime—and it could have been worse. What if that rock had hit you?"

"I was in bed, asleep. It was after midnight."

"That's not the point, Hannah, and you know it."

She sighed faintly and pursed her lips. She had that wall up around herself today; I could see it in her eyes.

I said, "I'd like to come in, if you don't mind."

"No, I don't mind."

She stood aside to let me enter, then closed the door and led me into the parlor. It had her stamp on it: oil paintings of garden scenes dominated by roses, new-looking banquet lamps with rose shades, rose-brocaded arm sleeves on a velveteen couch. I knew she was fond of roses; she grew them in her garden and often had vases of red and white buds on the porch tables. But there were other things here, too, such as a home graphophone and a cottage organ, that reminded me I did not know her well at all. She had never had occasion to tell me she was fond of music or that she played the organ. And I had never thought to ask if she had any such interests.

I went and looked at the rose-patterned carpet beneath the tacked-up piece of plywood. No glass shards, and no sign of the rock. I turned to face Hannah again.

"What did you do with the note?"

The question startled her. "How did you know there was a note?"

"Ervin Ramsey. I ran into him in town."

"But I didn't mention it in the message I sent him. . . ."

So then how did he know? I would ask him as soon as I was done here—with my fists, if necessary.

"Where is it, Hannah? I want to see it."

"I burned it."

"Why?"

"I don't want any more trouble, Lincoln."

"Neither do I—not for you or anybody else. But that means putting a stop to mischief like this, not ignoring it."

"Even if you find out who was responsible, it won't stop people from hating me. You must know that."

"I know that I have a job to do and that I'm going to do it," I said. "What did the note say?"

She was quiet for a time, back behind her protective wall. Then, abruptly, she said, " 'If you stay in Tule Bend, the next rock will break your head instead of your window.' That is what it said, word for word."

My chest was tight again. "And you say that's not important? That's a death threat, Hannah!"

"No. It's idle mischief. No one is going to hurt me."

"You can't be certain of that. There's a madman on the loose in this town. . . ."

"Oh, Lincoln, he isn't going to come after me. Did the killer write notes to his victims? Break their windows?"

"Who can tell what a madman will or won't do? Living up here all alone . . . you're vulnerable."

"Do you honestly believe I would be any less vulnerable living in the middle of town?"

I didn't intend to say the words, did not mean them, but they came out anyway: "There are other towns."

"Yes, there are other towns. I've lived in some of them—too many other towns. It has always been the same; it always will be the same for women like me."

"What do you mean, women like you?"

"You know what I mean. I am not going to run any more. This is my home and I intend to stay here. No one is going to drive me away, do you understand? No one."

Her eyes blazed for a few seconds; then she drew a deep breath and retreated once more behind her wall.

I said, "I don't want to drive you away, Hannah. Believe me, I don't. I'm only thinking of you, your safety."

"I know," she said.

"That rock and note . . . I feel responsible."

"Why should you?"

"It may have been done on account of me. There has been talk in town. About my visiting you evenings . . . scandalous talk."

"I see. And the ones doing the talking think you have been spending too much time with me, at the expense of your duties."

"Yes."

"You can't help what they think. It isn't your fault. People are frightened and they don't care who they blame for their fear."

"I don't care if they blame me. It's you I'm concerned about, Hannah."

"You needn't be. I'll be fine."

"Isn't there anywhere you can go for a few days, until we've got that madman in jail?"

"No, Lincoln. I've no more family, and no friends— nowhere to go at all."

"You could spend a few days in Petaluma or perhaps San Francisco. . . ."

"I'd rather not."

"Hannah . . ."

"Yes, I know, I am being stubborn. But I told you, I won't run away any more. Now you mustn't worry about me. I have a pistol and I know how to use it. I can take care of myself."

There was no arguing with her. And it was not my place to make any demands. I said reluctantly, "All right. If that's the way it has to be."

For a space we were both silent. Outside I could hear the wind rattling shingles and whistling under the eaves, as if it were playing games with the house.

Hannah asked then, "Do you think I'm a hard woman?"

"Hard? Why do you ask that?"

"The town thinks I am."

"Well, I don't."

"Even though I say I can take care of myself, that I don't need a man to do it for me?"

"Stubbornness," I said, "not hardness."

"A little of both, perhaps. I have seen enough of life— and enough of death—to put steel into me."

"Death?"

"My second husband killed two men while I was married to him," she said softly. "At least two, and the last one in cold blood."

I stared at her.

"He was the man I saw hanged in Kansas," she said. "Daniel Philip Tarboe was his name."

"My God." They were the only words that came to me.

"He was a gambler," Hannah said. "A good one but not good enough, according to his lights. He found it necessary to cheat." She paused, and then said, "You've heard the rumors about my . . . fall from grace. Some of them are quite true."

"I've never asked, Hannah."

"But you've wondered."

"Yes. I've wondered."

"I met Mr. Tarboe in Saint Louis," she said. "I was still married to George Weems then. George was the traveling man who . . . the father of my child, the man I ran off with. I left him for Mr. Tarboe. I would have left him eventually in any case. He was fickle and careless and there was nothing more between us."

"And the child?"

"My daughter. Samantha. She died of scarlet fever in her second year."

She had emerged from behind the wall again, the real Hannah, the vulnerable Hannah. There was pain in her voice and in her face: she had loved her child deeply.

"So I divorced George Weems and married Mr. Tarboe," she said. "It was an exciting life he led and he was good to me—at first. But then he was caught cheating in a high-stakes poker game with the owner of a Mississippi River steamer company and all but run out of the city, and after that his luck turned bad and he grew mean. He took his meanness out on me . . . and before long on a man in El Paso who won five hundred dollars from him at faro. Mr. Tarboe shot the man dead."

"Was he tried for the shooting?"

"Yes. And acquitted on his claim of self-defense. We left Texas soon after and traveled to Nebraska and then to Kansas. There was a fight in a resort in Bent Fork—another man accused Mr. Tarboe of cheating at cards. Mr. Tarboe shot him dead, too. This time, his claim of self-defense fell on deaf ears; he was convicted of willful murder and sentenced to hang. He did not die with dignity. He died weeping and begging for his life."

There was another silence while I tried to frame words. At length I said, awkwardly, "You must have loved him to stand by him to the end."

"No, you're wrong," Hannah said. "I did not stand by him—or love him any longer. I stayed in Bent Fork to see him hanged because I had no money and just enough pride left not to come crawling home to my father. I wish now, with all my heart, that I had. Pa never stopped loving me, despite the things we said to each other before I left Tule Bend with George Weems. I should have known that."

"How long did you stay in Bent Fork?"

"Four months. Long enough to earn enough money in a laundry to return to Saint Louis."

"Why Saint Louis?"

"It was a place I knew, with people I knew who would help me find decent work for decent wages. For two years I was a seamstress and milliner's helper. There were no other men in my life; have been none since Mr. Tarboe. The rumor mongers are wrong about that. I might still be in Saint Louis, living alone and working long hours, if word hadn't reached me of my father's death and his bequest."

"You could have had the house and property sold and the money sent to you in Saint Louis," I said. "Why did you decide to come back to live here instead?"

"I told you—I was weary of running away. I wanted—needed—familiar surroundings again. And this is my home, the only real home I've ever known."

I said nothing, because there was nothing to say. But Hannah misinterpreted my lack of response.

"Hardly a pretty tale, is it?" she said.

"Is anyone's life so pretty when you strip it to the bare bones?"

"Perhaps not."

"Hannah . . . why did you tell me all that?"

"You're the only person in Tule Bend who has treated me decently since I came back," she said. "The only person who seems to care. I didn't want you to wonder any longer."

"Knowing or not knowing . . . it doesn't make any difference in how I look at you."

"I'm glad. Thank you, Lincoln."

I felt the awkwardness again, and to cover it I said, "I had best be going now. Ervin Ramsey will be along directly and I want to talk to him before he starts work on your window."

"Just as you say."

"Will you let me know right away if anything else . . . unpleasant happens? At least promise me that."

"Yes. I will."

"Well, then. I'll call again soon, if I may."

"You're always welcome. I believe you know that."

"Tonight, perhaps. Or tomorrow night."

An odd little smile—one I could not quite read—moved her lips briefly and then was gone. "Yes," she said. "Tonight or tomorrow night. Any night at all."

CHAPTER 16

WHEN I got to the bottom of the bluff, Ervin Ramsey was just pulling his glass wagon off Tule Bend Road. I waited for him, raised my hand when he neared and called out for him to stop. Then I asked him, straight out, how he had known there was a note tied to the rock chucked through Hannah's window.

It took him aback; he was more mean than bright. But he covered up by saying, "I heard somebody say it."

"Who?"

"I don't recall."

"Where?"

"On Main. Somebody on Main this morning."

"Well, hear this," I said. "If I find out it was you wrote that note and threw that rock, I'll not only put you in jail, I'll chew on you like a rabid dog. And the same goes if there are any other incidents involving Miss Dalton."

"Can't hold me responsible for what somebody else does," he said sullenly.

"No? Well, if you hear somebody else making plans along those lines, you had better step right in and put a stop to it. Because you're the one I'll be coming after if you don't."

I left him to stew in his own juices and walked back into town fast and hard, to take the edge off my anger. A detail of nearly a dozen men and boys, half a dozen wagons, and a couple of sling-harnessed draft horses were laboring under Bert Lawless's supervision to clear away the wreckage of the three burned-out buildings. They had made considerable progress already; the site would be ready for rebuilding to begin within a week. One of the workers was Sam McCullough, I noticed—up and around in spite of his injuries from the falling roof beam. I drifted over to where he was moving stiffly through what had once been his saddlery shop, using a pry bar to poke among the ashes and charred fragments.

He had taken his loss hard. His face was etched with pain and fatigue lines and his eyes were hound sad. When I asked him how he was feeling he said, "Leg's all right but the cracked ribs are giving me hell. I can't hardly breathe."

"Lucky thing that beam didn't hit you a more solid lick."

"Lucky? Chrissake, Linc, my whole livelihood went up in that fire. Eight thousand dollars worth of saddles and harness and tools . . . everything I had. Been better if that beam had taken my head clean off and put me out of my misery."

"Come on, now, Sam, it's not that bad. Waldo Thomas will let you have a bank loan to rebuild. Won't be so long before you're back in business. Inside of six weeks, if the rains hold off."

"Won't be the same," he said morosely. "And I won't be out of debt again until the day I die." Then a thought seemed to occur to him that narrowed his eyes and put the shine of anger in them. "I heard it was that Emmett Bodeen set the fire. That true, Linc?"

"Far as we know, it is."

"Well, he better not come back to Tule Bend. If he does I'll kill him."

I said with pure honesty, "No need for that. He won't get away with his crimes—you have my word."

"Your word don't seem to be worth much these days."

"Soft, now. Friends sniping at friends doesn't do anybody a damn bit of good."

"Ah, Christ," he said, but his voice had gone dull again. He was not really one of those who were blaming me.

I asked him, "You heard about Morton Brandeis, Sam?"

"I heard."

"Odd, wouldn't you say?"

"Reckon."

"You and he are good friends. Any idea where he went or why?"

"No. Morton is close-mouthed, you know that."

"Never mentioned anything to you—any plans he might have, or any trouble?"

"No."

"He drew out half the money in his bank account before he left," I said. "More than three thousand dollars."

Sam frowned at that. "The hell he did. That sounds like he don't intend to come back."

"Sure does."

"Never said a thing to me, not a thing. Never offered condolences after the fire, never said goodbye. That's a hell of a way for a friend to behave."

I agreed that it was.

"You talk to Luke Preston?" he asked. "Luke's thicker with Morton than I ever was."

Luke Preston ran a gunsmith shop out of his house on Rollins Road, just north of town. I said, "Not yet, but

I will. Let me know if you hear anything about Morton, will you? And keep your chin up."

"Sure," he said. "Sure."

I walked up through town. Busy day, like most days in Tule Bend. Folks hurrying along the sidewalks, hunched against the brine-sharp wind; farm and dray wagons maneuvering into and out of Main Street; plenty of activity along the basin, too, where three heavily laden scow schooners and the last of the regular steamers that plied the creek—the little sternwheeler *Petaluma*—were in on the morning tide. But there was a difference in the bustle today—a tenseness, a kind of collective fear that you could see in the way people moved and talked, could almost smell coming off them. Men and women I had known all my life slipped past me without a word, a smile, or a nod. And on the faces of a few I saw thinly veiled hostility—as if I were an accessory to the murders, rather than one of the men who were trying to put an end to them.

On north Main, the saloons were doing a brisker business than usual for a weekday afternoon. There was a small crowd outside the Swede's, and as I passed by on the opposite side of the street I saw why: Joe Perkins was holding court, on the pretense of doing the job he was elected to do. He did not see me and nobody in the crowd noticed me either; I quickened my pace to make sure of it. My getting involved over there would only have brought some of the veiled hostility out into the open.

The trek to Rollins Road netted me nothing at all. Luke Preston wasn't home; his apprentice said he had taken the train to Santa Rosa for the day, to bid on some handguns that were being sold at auction. I told the youngster to tell Luke when he got back that I wanted to see him. Then, taking a roundabout route to avoid north Main, I paid my second visit of the day to Morton Brandeis's house on First Street.

When I got there Maude Seeley was just coming out of the front gate, all dressed up and wearing her ostrich plume hat. She didn't see me in time to scoot back inside. What she did do, though, was close up like a longneck clam as soon as she laid eyes on me. You could see her do it: her thin mouth got thinner, her narrow little eyes got even more squinched up, and she tucked her chin down into the wrinkly skin on her neck. She wasn't much to look at at the best of times, but right now she reminded me of a mean and scrawny old hen with her feathers preened, defending a barnyard corner.

She said in a no-nonsense voice, "I have nothing to say to you about Mr. Brandeis. Neither has my sister."

"Why not? Why all the secrecy?"

"That is none of your affair."

"It is if there is mischief involved."

"Mischief? What do you mean, mischief?"

"Just what I said. Why did Morton leave town so suddenly?"

"I told you, Mr. Evans, I have nothing to say about that."

"He drew more than three thousand dollars out of the bank before he left," I said. "Did you know that?"

Apparently she didn't. Her mouth popped open and she made a little gurgling noise in her throat; then her mouth snapped shut again, into such a thin line this time she might have been born without lips.

"Well, Mrs. Seeley?"

She glared at me for two or three seconds, said, "I have an urgent appointment and I shan't be late," and stalked off down the sidewalk. I called out to her, but my voice only put more stiffness in her spine. There was nothing else I could do to stop her or make her talk to me; I stood there feeling vexed and watched her out of sight.

Morton, I thought, just what in hell did you go and do?

The four o'clock conference took place in the council chambers and was nothing more than a windy rehash of the morning session. Nobody had found out anything worth a tinker's damn, including the fact that Emmett Bodeen's corpse was lying on a table in Obe Spencer's embalming room. Perkins and the mayor prattled on like a couple of politicians at a voters' rally, Perkins still stumping for the use of deputies to conduct a house-to-house search. He about had Mayor Gladstone convinced he was right. All it would take was for either of them to get a sniff of the truth about Emmett Bodeen.

As it was, the meeting broke up after an hour or so without anything being resolved except that half a dozen armed deputies would patrol Tule Bend, beginning tonight. I had no objection to that. If nothing else, it would keep hotheaded citizens from forming vigilante patrols of their own.

I went straight home afterward, for the first time in two days. Wasn't any point in avoiding Ivy any longer and I needed a hot bath, clean clothes, a decent meal, and a good night's sleep. I endured a ten-minute tongue-lashing and what seemed to be an endless string of questions and opinions. When she started in on Hannah and what the gossips were saying about "that woman" and me, I told her flat-out to shut her mouth;

then I left her with it hanging open instead and went and had my bath.

Over supper Ivy said primly that she didn't know what to make of me lately, that I was rude and short-tempered and Mother must be turning over in her grave to hear the way her only son talked to his sister. I said, "That's a lot of damned nonsense and you know it," which put an end to the conversation. She did not say another word to me. I thanked the Lord for small favors.

After I finished eating I took a walk to smoke my pipe. The madman, Morton Brandeis, Hannah . . . my thoughts kept skipping back and forth from one to the other.

Just how badly was the murderer hurt? I had checked in with Doc Petersen before the four o'clock meeting; he'd had nothing suspicious to report. Could be that the madman had sought medical attention in Petaluma or some other town, though Joe Perkins had sent word to all doctors throughout the county. More likely, the man had either doctored himself or been treated by someone he felt he could trust. Was he bedridden, or able to get up and around? And if he *was* able to get around, had his bloodlust been satisfied by three victims or would he come prowling after a fourth?

Then there was Morton's disappearance. It puzzled everybody I had talked to; no one could or would shed any light on his motives. I knew he couldn't be the madman, and I could not bring myself to believe he was mixed up in the hangings. And yet, the possibility kept nagging at my mind. Why had he picked Monday morning, right after hearing the news about Jacob Pike, to pack up and skedaddle if he *wasn't* involved somehow?

And then there was Hannah. That threatening note

bothered me more than I cared to admit. Likely it was just idle mischief, as she'd suggested, but you could never be sure about a thing like that. I did not like the idea of her up there alone in that house, isolated as it was; even if she *was* handy with a pistol, she might not have the chance to use it if she were taken by surprise. She could scream her head off up there and nobody would hear her.

I thought about going to her place, checking on her, but I didn't do it. If anyone decided to break in on her, he would surely wait until long past midnight—and there was just no way I could stay up all night, every night, to guard her. Better not to bother her at all tonight, I decided. Best I get some rest, so I could face tomorrow's trials afresh.

I went back home, and a little while after that I went to bed and straight to sleep.

But not for long.

CHAPTER 17

SOMEBODY was shaking me and whispering in my ear in urgent tones. "Lincoln! Wake up! For mercy's sake, wake up!"

I struggled up out of a heavy sleep for the second time in less than a week. Into pitch blackness again, except that this time a pale blob was leaning over my bed. Hard fingers had hold of my shoulder, rocking me as if I were a colicked baby in a cradle.

"What the devil—"

"Ssh! Keep your voice down."

Ivy. I pushed her hand away and got up into a sit, wagging my head to clear out the webs of sleep. "What is it, what's the matter?"

"There is someone in the backyard. Lordy, I think he's trying to break inside the house."

"What!"

"Ssshh! Do you want him to hear you?"

I was wide awake now. I swung my legs off the bed, fetching Ivy an unintentional kick as I did so. She made a faint gasping noise and kicked me back, as if I had done it on purpose. That was Ivy for you: run from a prowler and attack her own brother.

"Where is he?" I asked her as I stood up and fumbled for my pants.

"At the back door. I got up to—" She broke off. Just couldn't bring herself to say that she had got up to use the chamber pot. "I happened to glance out the window and there he was, bold as brass and plain as day in the moonlight, running across the yard."

"Recognize him?"

"No, he had his head down." She drew a deep breath, let it out in a quavery sigh. "A big man, huge, and . . . oh my Lord, Lincoln, there is something wrong with his left arm!"

The muscles in my neck and shoulders bunched tight. But I was not surprised. I said, "You sure?"

"It was drawn in close to his body, as if it were bandaged. . . . He's the murderer, isn't he? He's come for us next!"

Not for us, I thought grimly. For me.

I had my pants on now, and buttoned at the waist so they wouldn't fall down. I did not bother with any other clothing; just made my way across the dark room to where my Starr .44 hung in its holster from a wall hook. I slid the weapon out, rotated the cylinder a notch to put a live round under the hammer.

Behind me Ivy whispered, "You be careful, Lincoln Evans. If anything happens to you . . ." She didn't finish that sentence, either, but her meaning was plain enough. She was more concerned for her own safety than she was for mine.

I said, "You stay here," and slipped out through the open door into the hall.

When I got to the landing I stopped to listen. Faint scraping sounds at the rear of the house, as if he might be trying to jimmy the lock on the back door. A storm of rage had begun to blow inside me, black and hot, like a firewind. Well, by God, I thought, let him come in. I'll put a hole in the son of a bitch and an end to all this right here and now.

Scrape, scrape. And then, as I started down the stairs,

the noises stopped and there were no others. Either he had got the door open or given up for some reason— and if he had given up, it was not likely he would stand around outside for very long.

The stairs were carpeted, and a good thing too. I got to the bottom in a hurry and without making any noise, swung around the newel post into the downstairs hall-way. I paused again there, in close to the coat closet under the staircase.

Silence . . . then a faint creaking. Footfall on a weak board? Or just the old house making one of its nightly settling groans?

I eased the single-action's hammer back to half-cock and went on down the hall, hugging the left-hand wall. There was some dilution of the darkness behind me in the foyer—moonshine through the parlor windows and the fanlight over the front door—but here in the pas-sage it was well-bottom black. That meant the hall door to the kitchen and the one nearer, on my right, that opened into the dining room were both shut. If I had been certain he was in the house, I would have waited where I was for him to come through one of those two doors. As it was I reckoned the best thing was for me to keep moving.

I passed the dining room door, to within a couple of paces of the kitchen door. That one opened inward to the hall, so I did not want to be too close to it if he was on the other side and fixing to walk through. I listened again. Silence. Creak. Silence. Impatience made me reach out with my free hand, turn the porcelain knob; the click of the latch seemed overloud in the stillness. With my back against the wall, I dragged the door toward me until I could peer around its edge.

A little moonlight spilled in through the window over

the sink, gleamed dully off the glass-doored wall cabi-
net—just enough to let me see shapes in the dark.
Icebox, stove, butcher block, the sink with its jutting
pump handle. And over by the door to the service
porch—

Three things happened pretty much at once: Something slammed into the door a few inches above my
head, wobbling it violently in my grasp, sending out a
spray of wood splinters; there was a hollow booming
crack; gunflame lit up the kitchen for an instant, letting
me see the crouching silhouette of a man behind it.

I went to one knee, still holding onto the door, and
fired at the flash. Missed him: the bullet screeched off
metal. There was a confusion of noises as the echoes of
the shots died away: banging, thudding, a cry from Ivy
upstairs, a tinny clattering that sounded like her washtub being kicked over out on the service porch.

On the run again, damn his black soul. No more fight
in him now that he knew I was both alerted and armed.
I shoved up to my feet. Powdersmoke was thick in there;
I had to fight down a cough as I stumbled into the
kitchen. Then, in the dark, I barked my knee on an
edge of the butcher block, so that I half fell into the wall
next to the porch door. When I regained my balance
and looked through I saw the bent shape of him pawing
at the back door. He made a good target but only for a
second; by the time I swung over into position to fire
again, he was through the door and down the steps into
the yard.

I plunged after him. Almost tripped again, this time
over the washtub he had dislodged, but managed to
reach the back door upright and leaned through it. He
was running diagonally across the yard, dodging
around Ivy's clothesline toward the deep shadows cast

by the privy and the fruit trees that grew beyond, at the rear of our property. I ached to trigger another round at him, did not give in to the impulse. The light was poor for accurate shooting and I was too wrought up to trust my aim anyway. And shots in the night, out in the open like this where the sounds would carry, would rouse the whole neighborhood and set off a panic.

Chill wind stung my face as I ran down the steps, on across the yard in pursuit. There was frost on the grass again this morning, a thin icing of it; it made the footing slick, numbed the soles of my bare feet. Forty yards ahead, he blended into the shadows behind the privy and for few seconds I could not locate him. Then, when I caught sight of him again, he was barreling through the gate into the alleyway that bisected the block between First and Second.

He would have a horse tied back there somewhere—a sorrel horse, sure as hell. The knowledge made me try to quicken my pace, and that was a mistake. My naked foot stubbed against something unyielding in the grass—a tree root or rock—and I staggered, lost my balance once more, and this time went down hard on my belly and skidded a few feet on the frost-slick grass. The bole of one of the apple trees brought me up in a heap. Panting, biting my lip against the stinging pain in my toes, I pulled my legs under me and leaned up against the tree. I still had hold of the revolver, for all the good it was likely to do me now. A wonder it hadn't gone off when I smacked the ground, with me on top of it when it did.

I could no longer see him as I limped to the gate. It was only after I bulled out into the alleyway that I saw him again, and by then it was too late. He had had his horse tethered under the black oak that grew at the edge of Reverend Balfour's property next door and he was already in the saddle, wheeling the animal out from under the low-hanging branches and away from where I stood. I dropped to one knee, aiming—but he was stretched out over the horse's neck, the way he had been in Donahue Landing, and just about out of pistol range besides. Even so, I had to fight myself to keep from taking a couple of wild cracks at him.

Where the hell were Joe Perkins's patroling deputies now that I needed them?

I remained in a kneel, cursing softly and steadily, until he pounded out of sight. He had more luck than a hutch full of rabbits—a crazy man's crazy luck. Hanged Jeremy Bodeen and Jacob Pike and knocked me on the head, all right here in town; shot it out with Emmett Bodeen, hanged Bodeen, took a shot at me in Donahue, and then rode Christ knew how far dripping blood from a bullet wound; came back into town tonight, hurt as he was, and broke into my house and made *another* attempt on my life in my own kitchen. And each and every time, he had not only got clean away but managed to do it without anybody getting close enough to identify him. It was the kind of lucky streak—and the kind of unmitigated gall—you can scarcely believe until you see it happen.

The night was quiet now; nobody had raised an alarm. The commotion had seemed louder than it actually was: the thick walls of the house had muffled the two shots and the banging around inside, and neither of us had made any loud noises during the chase across the yard. At least I had that much—along with his poor aim—to be thankful for.

When I stood up I was aware for the first time of how cold it was. The wind slashed through the thin material of my nightshirt; the icy ground sent shoots of chill through my bare feet. Shivering, I pushed back into my yard.

As I came around past the shed, hurrying, I saw that there was a light in the Balfours' upstairs bedroom and that the Reverend had his bald head poked out of the window. When he saw me he called down, "That you, Lincoln? What's going on?"

"Nothing to be concerned about, Reverend."

"Did we hear shooting?"

"No. No cause for alarm."

He was a meek old soul, despite his calling—or maybe on account of it. He liked the idea of trouble even less than the next man. "Well, if you say so . . ."

"Sorry to have disturbed you. Good night."

He said something else that I did not listen to as I went on into the house. The stench of powdersmoke was still strong in the kitchen; I opened the window over the sink to let in fresh air. I was hunting for matches to light the kitchen lamp when Ivy came in with her bedroom lamp flickering, reminding me again of a scrawny ghost in her virginal nightdress.

She was all a-twitter; there had not been this much thrill and terror in her life since her wedding night. "You're not hurt, Lincoln? Those shots . . ."

"Do I look all bloody?"

"Well, you needn't snap my head off. Did he get away?"

"Yes, Ivy, he got away."

"Did you see his face?"

"No."

"I saw you chasing him across the yard," she said. "Mercy! I thought I was going to have a seizure, I was so frightened."

I had nothing to say to that. I located the matches and lit the wall lamp. Ivy gasped when she saw the damage that had been done by the exchange of shots, not that there was much of it. The madman's bullet had put a splintered hole in the kitchen door and the one from my revolver had ruined the nickel-plated finish on her Acme range. And there were a couple of dents in her washtub, a rip in the back screen door, and marks around the main door latch where he had pried it open.

But Ivy took it hard, as she had every right to. She followed me around making clucking, whimpering sounds, and when I was done with the inspection she said, "Oh, Lincoln, he was right here in our house—a crazy man with a gun! If I hadn't woken up he would have murdered us both in our beds!"

She has always had an irrational fear of being murdered in her bed. Why it should be more terrible to be murdered in your bed than anywhere else is beyond me. I said, "Now, Ivy. You did wake up, and neither of us is hurt."

"What if he comes back?"

"He won't. He's long gone by now."

"I don't mean tonight. What if he comes tomorrow night, or the next night, or—"

"He won't," I said again. "He is not going to walk around free much longer, I promise you that. By God, he's not."

She let out a shuddery sigh and clasped her hands at her breast. "I shall never feel the same about his house again," she said. "No, never. It was a *violation,* what he did tonight—a violation of home and hearth. . . ."

"That's foolishness."

"I mean it, Lincoln. I shall never feel safe here again!"

"Stop tormenting yourself and come along to bed."

"I shan't rest," Ivy said. "I shall never sleep well again."

She was being dramatic, as was her nature, but knowing that did not make me feel any less brotherly toward her. I patted her shoulder, went to secure the back door with a piece of wire. Then we climbed the stairs and went to our rooms in silence.

But I did not sleep, any more than Ivy was sleeping in her room. I lay there in the dark, my revolver close to hand, hating him and thinking about him coming here tonight. There could be no doubt that for some time now he had intended me to be one of his victims. But why? It was not just that he had recognized me in Donahue; there was some other reason, some wrong he believed I had done him. Whatever it was, his hate for me was as strong as it had been for the others he'd killed, as strong as mine was for him—strong enough to bring him after me in the middle of the night even though he was wounded.

Why Emmett Bodeen? Why Jacob Pike? And why me?

CHAPTER 18

MATTERS on all fronts began to come to a head in the morning, like boils that had grown ripe overnight and were finally ready to be lanced.

Instead of going to my office first thing, as I usually do, I rode my bicycle out to Rollins Road to see Luke Preston. He was already at work in his gunsmith shop, and he gave me a chagrined look when I walked in. He was a gnarly little man, feisty as a red rooster, who knew more about handguns and rifles and their loads than any man I had ever met. He was also as garrulous as Morton Brandeis was taciturn, which in a way explained why they were such close friends.

"I got your message, Linc," he said. "I would have been over to see you later on."

"Well, now I've saved you the trouble."

"It's about Morton, I suppose."

"Yes. You shed any light on his disappearance?"

"Well . . . might be I can. Don't know if I should, though. What he told me he told in confidence and I ain't a man to break a confidence."

"Special circumstances here," I said. "If you know where he is, you'd better tell me."

"What special circumstances?"

"The murders."

"Hell's fire, you don't suspect Morton . . ."

"Depends on what you tell me."

"All right, then. He knowed he couldn't keep it a

secret much longer anyway. He's been keepin' company with another woman."

"Another— Morton?"

"Been goin' on a couple of months now," Luke said. "Only told me a week ago. Bustin' to tell somebody. Man can't keep a thing like that locked up inside, not if he's got any decency left."

"Who's the woman?"

"Clemmie Abbott."

I said, surprised, "I'll be damned."

"My words exact when he told me."

Clemmie Abbott was a widow who lived with her mother and two kids on a small sheep ranch out at Stage Gulch. Quiet and hardworking, that was Mrs. Abbott; never any scandal connected with her that I knew about. But she was pretty, and probably lonely for a man—her husband had been gone two years now, dead of consumption—and it was easy enough to see how she could be attracted to Morton and vice versa.

"The Abbott place," I said. "That must be where he went."

"Reckon so. He didn't tell he was goin' to run off like he done, or I'd of tried to talk some sense into him."

"Must have been Jacob Pike's murder that drove him to it."

"Damfool thing to do, no matter what drove him to it," Luke said. "But sure, the Abbott place is where he went, all right."

"Is he still out there, that's the question."

"Well, Clemmie Abbott's got a mother and two kids to look after. Ain't likely she'd abandon them and her ranch to go somewheres else with Morton, now is it?"

"No," I said, "it isn't."

"He's still there," Luke said. "You can bet your last dollar on it."

I left him to his gunsmithing and pointed myself toward the Odd Fellows Hall and my office. Morton Brandeis and Clemmie Abbott. Wouldn't Ivy and her cronies have a picnic when they heard about it! Maude Seeley must have known about Morton and Mrs. Abbott, even if Lucy didn't; and she knew Ivy and her gossipy ways. No wonder she had been so unwilling to talk to me. And no wonder she had been so taken aback when I told her about Morton drawing out half the money in his and Lucy's bank account. It meant—and no doubt of it—that he planned not to come back to Tule Bend.

A coward's way of avoiding responsibility and unpleasantness, that was the sum total of Morton's actions. And it lowered my estimation of him by a goodly margin. Just went to prove again, if I needed any more proof, that you could know a man all your life and not really know him at all.

I was a block from the Odd Fellows Hall when I heard my name called and spied Boze running toward me from down toward Main. I stopped peddling to wait for him. He was red-faced and panting, as if he had been running a race. Which was just what he had been doing—a race with me as the prize.

"I been lookin' all over for you, Linc," he said when he had his breath. "We got trouble."

"Now what?"

"Perkins found out about Emmett Bodeen. I don't know how but he did."

"Shit!"

"He's lookin' for you too. Tried to buttonhole me about it, but I pretended I didn't know a thing."

"The mayor know too?"

"If he doesn't, he will any minute."

I did some rapid thinking. "Well, we're not going to be here for either of them to wipe their boots on. Not until tonight, anyhow."

"How come? Where we goin'?"

"Out to Stage Gulch to have a talk with Morton Brandeis."

"Morton? What's he doin' out there?"

"I'll fill you in on the way. About something that happened last night, too."

We managed to get our horses out of the Union Hotel stables, and them and ourselves across the Basin Draw-bridge and out of town, without running into Perkins or any of his deputies. There were knots of men milling restlessly outside the saloons on north Main and those over by the S.F. & N.P. yards, which meant that word of Emmett Bodeen's murder had already begun to spread. I had sworn Ivy to secrecy about last night, but still she might let something slip; and if she did, that news would only fan the flames.

In any case there was nothing Boze or I could do about public unrest. The mayor would be in Perkins's corner now, with both of them mad as hell at me, so the problem was theirs. Whether Boze and I stayed in town today or not, it was a good bet neither of us would have our city jobs waiting for us by nightfall.

Frustration rode with me all the way out to Stage Gulch. A bitter feeling of failed responsibility, too. If I had managed to put a bullet in that son of a bitch last night, the town would not be a powderkeg today and we would not be facing the scorn and anger of everybody in it. I tried to tell myself I had done what I thought was right, in everyone's best interest. Tried to tell myself, too, that maybe Morton Brandeis knew something, no matter how small, about the murders. But none of that held off a galled suspicion that here I was doing the very thing Morton had: running away.

The Abbott ranch buildings were tucked back in a cleft where two low hills folded against each other. Sheep graze spread out in front of them, supporting over two hundred black-faced woolies. It was a pretty little place, with shade trees around the house and a stream that meandered nearby. Clemmie Abbott had managed to keep it up since her husband's death, thanks to the efforts of her two boys and a pair of hired hands.

It was coming on noon when we drew rein in front of the ranchhouse. The youngest of the Abbott boys, who was about twelve, was over in the shearing pens; he stopped what he was doing to watch us approach but he did not come near us. It wasn't until I hailed the house that we saw anyone else. And at that it took half a minute for Mrs. Abbott to appear.

She was a sweet-faced woman; the years of hard toil did not seem to have taken much of a toll, even though she was near forty. Dressed as she was now, in a man's Levi's and a linsey-woolsey shirt, with her brown hair gathered back into a couple of braided tails, she looked ten years younger than her age.

"Morning, Mrs. Abbott."

"Mr. Evans. What can I do for you?"

"I think you know why we're here," I said. "We're looking for Morton Brandeis."

"Why would you think he's here?"

"We know he is and there's no good pretending otherwise. If he's in the house, ask him to come on out. If he's somewhere else, you'd best tell us where."

She hesitated. But she did not have to make up her mind one way or the other; Morton made it up for her. He came out of the shadows inside the house, walking slow, and stopped beside her and put his arm around her shoulders in a way that was both possessive and defiant. He didn't look defiant, though. He looked tired and a little haggard, as if he had not been sleeping well lately; as if his conscience might be bothering him some.

"So you found out," he said.

"Only a matter of time, Morton."

"Who told you? Maude or Luke Preston?"

"Luke."

"Shouldn't have told him. I knew that but I did it anyway."

"Had to come out sooner or later."

He studied me for a few seconds, then shifted his gaze to Boze. There was a set disapproval on Boze's face—the news had dealt him a harder jolt than it had me—and I suppose some of my feelings showed on mine too. Morton's arm tightened around Mrs. Abbott's lean shoulders.

"Clemmie and me, we love each other," he said, the defiance in his voice now. "I'm not going to apologize for it. It happened and that's that."

"You might have waited," I said.

"Until Lucy passes on? Yes, I might have. But that could be a year or more and I . . . Linc, I couldn't stand it any more, there in that house with her dying by inches and that sister of hers harping at me all the time. When I heard about Pike, when that got heaped on my back too . . . Christ, a man can only take so much!"

"Morton is entitled to some peace and happiness," Mrs. Abbott said. "Everyone is."

"What about Lucy's peace?" Boze said thinly. "You

reckon she'll have any now, lyin' there so sick and knowin' her husband deserted her for another woman?"

Morton said, "She don't care about me any more. Neither of them do. Lucy and me . . . even before she got sick, it was finished between us. We hardly said a private word to each other in more than a year."

"She's still your wife. And she's *dying*."

Morton's mouth set tight. "I been all through that with myself and with Clemmie. My mind's made up— I'm staying right where I am. I talked to a lawyer in Petaluma about a divorce and putting the livery up for sale. Lucy can have the house. So if you come to try talking me into going back, you're wasting your time."

"You do whatever you have to do, Morton," I said. "That's between you and your conscience."

"Then why're you here?"

"The hangings. Three of 'em now."

"Three? Lord, Linc, I don't know anything about it. What makes you think I do?"

"I didn't say I thought you did. You hear of anybody suffered a gunshot wound recently, left arm or shoulder?"

"No. Why?"

"Never mind why. You, Mrs. Abbott?"

"No," she said.

"Morton, you have any idea why Jacob Pike was killed?"

"I've thought about that," he said. "No. It don't make any sense to me."

"He have any trouble with anybody lately?"

"Not that I know about."

"Seem worried or nervous to you?"

"No. Same as he always was."

I fished the presidential medal out of my pocket;

Boze had returned it to me yesterday and I had been carrying it ever since. "You ever see this before? Or one like it?"

Morton took the medal, studied on it for a few seconds. "Where'd you get it?" he asked.

"Found it in the livery Monday morning. Whoever killed Pike likely dropped it. *Have* you seen one like it?"

I expected him to say no, just as everyone else had. Instead he said, "Matter of fact, I have."

I stared at him, coming tight inside. There seemed to be a sudden crackly feel in the air, the same kind as when an electrical storm is about to break.

"In Tule Bend?"

"In my livery not long back. Man was paying me for some work I done and he pulled this out of his pocket by mistake. Said it was a good-luck charm."

"What man? Name him."

And Morton said, "Jubal Parsons."

CHAPTER 19

IT was after two by the time we reached the rutted trail that hooked up to the Parsons' farm. Just inside the gate, I drew rein; and when Boze followed suit I said, "You sure you want to go through with this?"

"We already talked it out," he said.

And we had, on the ride in from the Abbott ranch. We could have gone straight into Tule Bend, rounded up Joe Perkins and his deputies, come back out here in force. But that was not the way to do it. Just because Jubal Parsons owned a presidential medal did not mean the one I'd found was his or he was the madman. Tell Perkins about it, let him lead a manhunting posse when feelings were already running at fever pitch, and there was liable to be the kind of consequences where innocent people got hurt.

No, this was the right way to do it: one or two men, taking it slow and cautious. It was my job—and I had a vested interest in the outcome anyhow, for more reasons than one—but Boze was only a part-time deputy, with no personal stake except maybe the saving of that part-time job. He did not have to put his life at risk, not with a wife and two kids waiting at home and not on a mission like this one.

I said as much to him now, for the second or third time: "You don't have to do this."

"You think I'm goin' to let you go up there alone? Think again, Linc. We been friends too long."

"Sure?"

"Sure enough."

His jaw was set, white with bunched muscle below the mouth corners. His hands moved restlessly on the pommel of his saddle, but it was just a normal edginess; there was no scare in his eyes. Neither a hero nor a coward, that was Ed Bozeman. Just a man with a disagreeable task to do. And that was me too, I thought. I could trust Boze and he could trust me, and more than that two men—two officers of the law—could not ask.

"All right," I said. "Let's get it done."

I made sure my revolver was loose in his holster and my coat was tucked back away from the butt; then we proceeded up the trail. As we rode, I thought that it was peculiar how things worked out sometimes. All corkscrewed and unpredictable. On the trek out from town I had been worried that I was running away from responsibility, and all along maybe I had been pointing toward it instead. It was such circumstances that made you believe in divine guidance.

And yet, on the other hand, Morton running off when *he* had might only have prolonged the outcome. If he had just stayed in town long enough on Monday morning for Boze to show him the medal, all the anguish of the past two days—the attempt on my life last night—might never have happened. Where was a divine hand in the actions of a coward and a lovestruck fool?

I thought about Jubal Parsons, too. The way he'd looked and acted on Sunday, the strangeness of him. But there was no way I could have suspected him for that alone. Plenty of men were strange, and none of them went around committing wanton murder. No, there was just no way for a reasonably sane man to

THE HANGINGS ■ 167

know, or to understand, what went on inside the head of a madman.

The sun had broken through the cloud cover but there was no warmth in it where it touched my back. A chill wind blew down off the mountains, carrying the creak and rusty flutter of the windmill to us long before we could see it. Needed grease and plenty of it, that mill. Had it been my responsibility, I would have tended to the greasing long ago; on windy days a steady screeching sound like that could fray your nerves. Just a few minutes of it, here and now, put an extra twist in the knot of tension between my shoulder blades.

We topped the low rise from where the farm buildings were visible. Someone was sitting on the farmhouse steps: Greta Parsons, the skirts of her dress billowing in the wind. There was no sign of Jubal Parsons, or at least none that could be seen from a distance. I laid my right hand on the Starr's handle as we continued downhill and into the farm yard. All the while that confounded windmill kept up its shrieking, loud and then soft, soft and then loud, like the souls of the damned pleading in endless torment.

Boze and I stopped our horses a few yards from where Mrs. Parsons was sitting. Her head had lifted at our approach, then lowered again to the cream separator on the ground before her. She still had her head down as she strained milk into the separator, placed a cream can under one spout and a bucket under the other, began to turn the crank.

I let my gaze rove the house, the yard, the other buildings. Still no indication of Jubal Parsons. But there was one thing I did see and take note of: Two horses stood in the pole corral out beyond the barn, one the ploddy gray that had been hitched to the farm wagon on my last visit and the other a sorrel saddle horse. I had not noticed the sorrel last week, if it had been there in the corral for me to notice. No reason I should have. Sorrel was a common color for a horse.

"Mrs. Parsons," I said, and waited until she raised her head again after a few seconds. Then I said, "We'd like a few words with your husband. Would he be in the house?"

"No. The barn."

"Alone, is he?"

"Oh yes. He has always been alone, that man."

There was an odd note in her voice—a kind of dull emptiness as if she were greatly fatigued. She moved that way, too, loose and jerky. She did not seem to notice the way Boze and I sat our horses, poised, hands laid on the handles of our sidearms. Or if she did notice, she didn't seem to care.

I asked, "Mind saying if he has been hurt recently, left arm or shoulder?"

"Shot, you mean. Yes, someone shot him."

Boze and I exchanged glances. No more question now: Jubal Parsons was our man. I let my gaze shift sideways to the barn. The doors appeared to be shut tight and so did the loft door above. There was a window on the near side but it, too, was closed.

"How bad is his wound?" I asked her.

"Very bad," she said, and for an instant something that might have been the ghost of a smile twitched at her lips. "Very, very bad."

"Then . . . why is he in the barn and not the house?"

"I wouldn't let him stay in the house. No more, I said, no more. I told him he'd have to sleep in the barn until you came for him. That is where he has been ever since

. . . except for last night. He went away late last night and came back just before dawn."

She knows, I thought. But hell, how could she *not* know?

"Is he armed?"

"Yes, but you needn't worry. He won't use his weapons against you."

"How do you know that?"

"I just know."

"Is he unconscious?"

"You can walk right in," she said, as if she had not heard me. "It's all right. You haven't anything to fear."

I traded another look with Boze. Then we both stared over at the barn again.

"Truly," Mrs. Parsons said. And then lowered her head and once more began to turn the crank on the separator. The sound the crank made was like a miniature echo of the shriek of the windmill blades.

I could see no reason to disbelieve her. There was no sense in her trying to lead us into a trap. *She* wasn't crazy; she had to know that there would be others after us, that you can't murder everybody who poses a threat to you. No, it was not a trap. We had been sitting here close to five minutes now and nothing had happened. If Parsons was conscious he had likely heard us ride in; and if he was able to get up and around, he could have poked that rifle of his out through the barn door or loft door or side window, even with a crippled arm, and pumped a dozen bullets at us by now.

I dismounted, waited for Boze to do the same, then drew my revolver and headed slowly toward the barn. Boze drew, too, and fell into step beside me. There was no change on the face of the barn as we approached, nor anything to hear from inside. The smell of dust and earth and manure was ripe on the chill air.

I motioned to Boze that he should go over to the side window; he nodded, sheered off that way. I stepped around an old McCormick & Deering binder-harvester, came up to the closed doors. Still nothing to hear from inside, but then I would not have been able to make out soft sounds because of the wind and that banshee windmill.

No point in prolonging things: With my left hand I found the latch on the left door half and then yanked the door open, keeping my body out of the way against the right half. The sudden action drew no gunfire, brought no response of any kind. Even so, an oily flow of sweat trickled down from under my arms. I waited through a count of ten, then shouldered through the right door half, inside.

Still no response or resistance.

It was shadowed in there, even with the open doors; those parts of the interior that I could make out were empty. Outside the daylit rectangle of the window I saw Boze's face peering in. I moved forward a few paces, toward where the corn crib was.

Sudden sharp rapping noise from the direction of the window: knuckles on glass. Boze. When he had my attention he found purchase on the window sash, slid it up, and ducked his head underneath.

"She was right, Linc," he said heavily. "We got nothing to fear from Jubal Parsons."

"What do you mean?"

"Wait for me to come in."

I waited, and in a few seconds he was beside me again. "Over where that tack is hangin' under the loft," he said. "I had a good squint from the window."

He led me over that way. And what I saw put a slithery feeling on my back, the taste of metal on my tongue.

Jubal Parsons lay crumpled face-up on the sod floor, a Colt sidearm and rigging strapped at his waist, left arm held in tight against his body by soiled and blood-stained bandages. There was blood all over the front of his shirt and tan jacket, too; streaks of it on his neck and the side of his face. From the look of the blood he had been dead several hours. Shot dead, likely with the .45-70 Springfield rifle that lay beside the body; when Boze bent down and struck a match you could see the black-powder marks mixed up with the blood on his chest.

"Shot twice, looks like," Boze said.

"Which means that he didn't do it himself."

"Not hardly," he said.

Our eyes met in the dim light. Then we turned and crossed back to the doors. When we came out Mrs. Parsons was still sitting on the farmhouse steps, still working with the cream separator. We walked over and stopped in front of her. The sun was at our backs, and the way we stood put her in our shadow. That was what made her look up this time; she had not seen or heard us approaching.

She said, "Did you find my husband?"

"We found him," I said. "What happened, Mrs. Parsons?"

"I shot him," she said. Matter-of-fact, as if she was telling you the time of day. "This morning, right after he came back from wherever he went last night. Ever since I have wanted to hitch up the wagon and drive in and tell you about it, but I couldn't seem to find the courage. It took all the courage I had to fire the rifle."

"Why did you do it?"

"Because of what *he* did. All the terrible things he did."

"You knew all along? Last Sunday when I was here?"

"No, not all along." Then she blinked and said, "Well, that is not quite true. I suspected. I just wouldn't believe. I didn't *know* until he came back Monday evening, hurt the way he was, half out of his head. Then I asked him, straight out."

"And he told you?"

She did not answer right away. She was still fiddling with the separator and the cans, as if they were things— normal, familiar things—she couldn't bear to let go of. She had finished separating the cream; now she put the lid on the cream can and the bucket of skim milk to one side, and began taking the separator apart for washing.

I said, gently, "Mrs. Parsons?"

"Yes, he told me," she said. "He told me everything. That was when I made him go to the barn. That was when . . . that was . . ." She broke off, shaking her head, and her fingers grew even busier with the parts of the separator.

"Why did he hang Jeremy Bodeen?"

"He was crazy jealous, that's why."

"You mean to say you knew Bodeen before last week?"

"No. He was a stranger to me. The only time I ever saw him was that day, last Tuesday afternoon. He followed me up from Willow Creek Road. He said he was looking for work. I told him we had none, that we were tenant farmers, but he wouldn't leave. He kept following me around, saying things. He thought I was alone here—a woman alone."

"Did he . . . well, make trouble for you?"

"Touch me, you mean? No. Just words. Saying things, suggestive things. Men like that . . . I don't know why but they think I am a woman of easy virtue. It has always been that way, no matter where we've lived. A woman of easy virtue . . . I'm not, I am not, I have never once broken my marriage vows."

A knob of something seemed to have lodged in my throat, and the taste of it was more bitter than camphor. In my mind I could hear Ivy's voice, so self-righteous, so knowing, branding Greta Parsons—a woman she did not even know—as a common tramp, saying Greta Parsons was no better than she should be and certainly no better than that woman up on the hill, that trollop Hannah Dalton. And I could hear Hannah's voice, too, yesterday morning in her parlor, saying, *Yes, there are other towns. I've lived in some of them—too many other towns. It has always been the same; it will always be the same for women like me.*

Boze was asking, soft, "What did you do? About Bodeen?"

"Ignored him at first," Mrs. Parsons said. "Then I begged him to go away. I told him my husband was violently jealous but he didn't believe me. I also thought I was alone, you see. I thought Jubal had gone off to work in the fields."

"But he hadn't?"

"Oh, he had. But he came back while Bodeen was here and overheard part of what was said."

I asked, "Did he show himself to Bodeen?"

"No. He just watched and listened. After a while the drifter grew tired of tormenting me and went away. Then Jubal came out. He didn't say a word to me. He just saddled his horse and went away. Followed that man into Tule Bend and when he caught up with him after dark he struck him on the head and then he hanged him."

"Just for deviling you?" Boze said. "He murdered a man in cold blood just for that?"

"Yes. He did."

"And Jacob Pike?" I asked. "Why him?"

"The same reason."

"Pike was forward with you? Insulted you?"

She nodded. "Last Thursday, at the livery. When I went there looking for Jubal, that boy . . . he made a lewd suggestion. Veiled, but plain enough. Jubal must have heard; he walked in soon afterward."

Boze still wore his fuddled look. He said, "Why did he hang them? I don't understand the meanin' of that."

"You didn't know him," Mrs. Parsons said. "You just . . . you didn't know how he was. He used to say that if a man thought evil, and spoke evil, it was the same as doing evil. He said if a man was wicked, he deserved to die for his wickedness and the world would be a better place for his leaving it."

"Religious fanatic, then?"

"No. He was no more religious than most men. He was *moral*—a moral fanatic. He believed in absolute right and wrong, good and evil, with nothing in between. For a time after we were married, I admired that in him. There was no trouble then. But later . . . he changed. Almost before I knew it, he became a stranger. Part of it was the things people thought and said about me and to my face. He worshipped the ground I stand on—he truly did. He couldn't bear the thought of anyone sullying me. The other reasons why he changed . . . I don't know. He worked too hard, for so little. And he was inflexible—he did not know how to bend. A person has to know how to bend, like a sapling in the wind. You cannot survive unless you learn how to bend."

"You must have come to hate him," Boze said. "To do what you did."

"Not so much hate—fear. I was afraid of him and for him. He was so big, so strong-willed, and yet underneath so weak. I used to tremble sometimes just to look at him."

"Did he try to hurt you, is that it?"

She had finished dismantling the separator and was sitting now with her hands folded in her lap and her head bowed, like a child at a prayer meeting. "No," she said to her hands. "He hurt me but not the way you mean. He didn't once lay a hand to me the whole nine years we were married. It was what he was, what he became, that hurt me."

"Then why did you shoot him?"

"Three men already dead," she said, "and last night he went away to kill someone else." Her head came up partway. "Did he, Mr. Evans?" she asked me. "Kill someone last night?"

"He tried to," I said.

"But he didn't?"

"No."

"Thank God. Who was it?"

"Me," I said.

". . . I should have known. It must have been because you were here on Sunday, alone with me, and I gave you the Christmas candle. You must have mentioned it to him; he asked me about it that night, what made me give it to you. In his sickness he must have thought . . . no, it doesn't matter now what he thought."

I said nothing. There was nothing to say. A little innocent thing like the gift of a candle, and it had almost cost me my life; he had wanted to *hang* me for accepting it from her. It might have been funny if it were not so monstrous.

"When I heard him leave," she said, "I knew he was after another man. By the time I got the rifle it was too late to stop him, he was already gone. So I waited for him. I sat up until dawn, with the rifle on my lap, waiting, and when I heard him ride in I went to the barn and I shot him. I didn't give him a chance to speak, I just . . . shot him. As you would a rabid dog, to protect yourself and others and to put him out of his misery. You do understand, don't you?"

"Yes, Mrs. Parsons," I said. "We understand."

She looked away from us, out over the fields—and a long ways beyond them, at something only she could see. In the silence that windmill shriek was like the constant dabbing of saltpeter in an open wound.

After a time she said, "No roots—that was part of it too. What led him to do such terrible things. Moving here, moving there, always moving—three states and five homesteads in less than ten years. But . . . oh, the last two places, the two before we came here . . . I should have known. No, I *did* know but I wouldn't believe."

She wasn't making sense. Or I thought she wasn't until she said, "He held the job of private hangman a long time, Jubal did—a long time." She shifted position as she spoke, so that her face came out of shadow and into the sunlight. And what I saw in her eyes, as much as the next words she uttered, put a chill on my neck like the night wind does when it blows across a graveyard.

"Those men he killed here weren't the first," she said. "There were at least two others. God help me, at least two others . . . and how many more that I never heard about?"

CHAPTER 20

WE took Jubal Parsons' corpse back to town in his farm wagon, with Boze driving and Mrs. Parsons on the seat beside him. She sat very prim and stiff-backed, the way she had on the porch steps, with her hands folded in her lap. As far as I could tell, riding along behind with Boze's dun on a lead, she did not say a word all the way in.

It was dusk when we crossed the Basin Drawbridge. There was a restless crowd up near the Swede's on north Main, some of the men carrying lighted torches—always a bad sign. I rode up alongside the wagon, told Boze to stop and wait for me, and then gigged Rowdy up to where the crowd was milling. There were some jeers when they first saw me, but when I stood up in the stirrups and began shouting them down, telling them about Jubal Parsons, they quieted. By the time I finished there was a hush. In that hush I wheeled away, rode back to the wagon. And as we continued up to Main I saw that the crowd was already starting to break up, the men extinguishing their torches and filtering into the saloons in little groups.

We went first to Doc Petersen's and put Mrs. Parsons in his care. Then we drove to Spencer's Undertaking Parlor and delivered the dead man to Obe. And then we proceeded to the constable's office—which we found empty—and waited for word to get around to Mayor Gladstone and Joe Perkins.

It did not take long. Inside of twenty minutes both of them had arrived, along with all four members of the town council and quite a few others. Boze and I used up an hour in explanations and answering questions. Everyone seemed satisfied then, except Perkins; he was miffed because he reckoned we had stolen thunder that was rightfully his. He all but accused me outright of being after his job, and when I laughed in his face he stormed out. The mayor was so relieved that he failed to chastise me for keeping Emmett Bodeen's death a secret from him. Nobody else said anything about it, either. My job and Boze's were safe.

When the meeting finally broke up Boze went home to his wife and kids and the others went home to their families. There would be plenty of talk tomorrow and on through the week, but then it would die down and things would settle back to normal. The hangings were destined to be more than just a thrilling memory for some, though: Morton Brandeis, Lucy Brandeis, Maude Seeley. Boze and me. Maybe Ivy, too. For Greta Parsons, they would always be a nightmare. And it would be a long time before her life settled back to normal, if it ever did again.

I did not go home like the other men. There was something I had to do first—something I should have done weeks ago.

With Rowdy under me, I rode south out of town and on up the hill to the Dalton house. Hannah was sitting on the enclosed part of the porch tonight, in deference to the cold, her hair done up and fastened with a comb like usual and a green shawl over her shoulders. Her welcoming smile warmed me. And for the first time, as I sat beside her, I did not feel a trace of awkwardness in her presence.

When I told her about Jubal and Greta Parsons I could see that she felt the tragedy of it in the same way I did, and that it made her sad. She and Mrs. Parsons were so much alike. Both wronged in so many ways; both forced to live with death, to watch men they had once loved commit murder and then suffer the consequences of their acts. Good women, trying to live decent lives but trapped by poor judgment on the one hand and the actions and malicious gossip of fools on the other.

Yes, and in Hannah's case one of the fools was me. In my own selfish fashion I had done her as much of an injustice as Ivy and her ilk. Sneaking up here after dark to see her, and pretending to everyone else that I wasn't; worried about *my* reputation, about keeping up appearances. Only once had I come calling during the daytime—yesterday morning, on business. I recalled that odd little smile just before I left her yesterday, and the way she had said, "Tonight or tomorrow night. Any night at all." Now I knew what both the smile and the words really meant.

On the way here I had worked out how I would say all of this to her. It was not easy, getting the words to come, but once I had some of them trickling out—the pump primed—the rest came spilling free in a rush. I asked her to forgive me for being such a blind fool. I asked her to permit me to call on her during the day as well as in the evening; I said I would admire to take her to supper now and then, to socials at the Odd Fellows Hall, on picnics and other outings.

I watched her face closely as I spoke. And I saw the shape of her expression change, grow softer; I saw part of her wall begin to crumble. Then, when she asked, "Are you speaking as a suitor, Mr. Evans?" and I said,

"Yes, I am, Miss Dalton," I saw the rest of the wall collapse and I knew that what the poor ugly duckling had never dared to hope for had been within close reach all along.

Hannah said, "But are you sure it's what you want? There will be those who shun you, just as they shun me. . . ."

"Let them. It's you I care about, not this blasted town or most of the people in it. If I had found the courage I would have declared myself long ago. But I scarcely found enough to admit my feelings to myself."

She reached out and touched my hand, let her fingers rest there. "You aren't the only one who lacked courage," she said.

"Then your answer is yes?"

"My answer is yes."

"There'll be no more delays, then. Tomorrow at noon, with you dressed in your finest, we'll stroll arm in arm down Main Street, have lunch at the Union Hotel, then take coffee at my home so I may present you to my sister Ivy."

"Won't she be delighted?" Hannah said, and laughed.

I laughed with her, thinking of Ivy's face when I walked in with Hannah on my arm. It was good to laugh again and to feel this much happiness, even though it had taken three deaths and another woman's bitter tragedy to bring it about. But that was the way of things. Good sometimes grows out of the worst calamity, and the true fools are those who fail to embrace it when it comes their way.

Without planning to I kissed her, as if I had taken such a liberty many times before. Turned out to be as easy and natural as winking your eye. And even sweeter than I ever imagined it would be.

AUTHOR'S NOTE

THE locale of this novel is, for the most part, authentic. In 1892 the physical characteristics of Petaluma Creek (now Petaluma River, by a 1959 act of the California state legislature) were as I've depicted them; so was its use as a busy shipping lane to and from San Pablo and San Francisco bays. The creek, in fact, was of major import in the development and settlement of the area some fifty miles north/northeast of San Francisco, and at one time carried more traffic than any California watercourse except the Sacramento and San Joaquin rivers. The town of Petaluma is most certainly real: I was born and raised there. So are Lakeville, Stage Gulch, and such places mentioned in passing as Santa Rosa, Sonoma, Glen Ellen, and the Valley of the Moon. Donahue Landing has long since disappeared, but its birth and death were as recorded here, and in 1892 it was very much a blot on the creekside landscape (though I confess to having taken a few liberties with its physical makeup at that time).

An incident similar to the one presented in the first chapter may or may not have actually occurred in Petaluma in 1856: a stranger was allegedly found hanging by the neck from the framework of an artesian well on Main Street. The Petaluma *Journal* speculated that the man either committed suicide or was a criminal executed by vigilantes (who were a force in Sonoma County in those years, just as they were in San Francisco). But

local historians tend to discredit the report as an elabo-
rate practical joke, perhaps perpetrated by the staff of
the *Journal*. My extrapolation of and explanation for
such a bizarre occurrance is entirely fictitious.

Also fictitious is the town of Tule Bend. There is not
nor has there ever been a town on the creek a few miles
south of Petaluma. At one time there *was* a steamboat landing, known as Haystack Landing or "The
Haystacks," but it never evolved into anything more
substantial.

While California had its fair share of madmen in the
nineteenth century, none of them—at least so far as I
know—suffered from the sort of neck-stretching mania
that afflicted Jubal Parsons. Parsons, Lincoln Evans,
Hannah Dalton, and all the other characters portrayed
on-stage in these pages are figments of my imagination.
Only General Mariano Vallejo and Peter Donahue are
actual historical figures.